Betrayed

Patricia H. Rushford

D0980397

Jennie McGrady Mystery Series

Helen Bradley Mystery Series

Betrayed

Patricia H. Rushford

BETHANY HOUSE PUBLISHERS
MINNEAPOLIS, MINNESOTA 55438

Published by Bethany House Publishers
A Ministry of Bethany Fellowship, Inc.
11300 Hampshire Avenue South
Minneapolis, Minnesota 55438

Printed in the United States of America.

Library of Congress Cataloging-in-Publication Data

Rushford, Patricia H.
    Betrayed / Patricia Rushford
      p.   cm. — (The Jennie McGrady mystery series ; 7)
      Summary: Jennie begins detective work when she arrives at the ranch owned by her uncle, a full-blooded American Indian, and learns that an explosion has killed one man and severely injured another.

    [1. Ranch life—Fiction. 2. Nez Percé Indians— Fiction. 3. Indians of North America—Fiction. 4. Mystery and detective stories.] I. Title. II. Series: Rushford, Patricia H. Jennie McGrady mystery series ; 7.
PZ7.R8972Be   1996
[Fic]—dc20   95–43935
ISBN 1–55661–560–4   CIP
                                         AC

Dedicated to Jan Bono
and her sixth-grade class
at Hilltop Elementary
in Illwaco, Washington.

PATRICIA RUSHFORD is an award-winning writer, speaker, and teacher who has published numerous articles and over twenty books, including *What Kids Need Most in a Mom*, *The Humpty Dumpty Syndrome: Putting Yourself Back Together Again*, and her first young adult novel, *Kristen's Choice*. She is a registered nurse and has a master's degree in counseling from Western Evangelical Seminary. She and her husband, Ron, live in Washington State and have two grown children, six grandchildren, and lots of nephews and nieces.

Pat has been reading mysteries for as long as she can remember and is delighted to be writing a series of her own. She is a member of Mystery Writers of America, Sisters in Crime, Society of Children's Book Writers and Illustrators, and several other writing organizations. She is also co-director of Writer's Weekend at the Beach.

1

"We've begun our final descent to Missoula." The pilot thanked them for flying with Horizon and added, "Looks like clear skies and eighty degrees."

Jennie twisted her long dark braid and peered at the rugged wilderness below. Butterflies soared through her stomach again as she thought of her aunt and uncle and the trouble they'd been having at the Dancing Waters Dude Ranch.

Take it easy, McGrady, Jennie told herself for the umpteenth time since leaving Portland. *You're getting worked up over nothing.* Aunt Maggie had called the explosion an accident. But what if she was wrong?

Since she'd often been accused of having an overactive imagination, Jennie blotted out the questions and focused instead on the snow-capped peaks and forest below.

"Ever been to Montana before?" the young man sitting beside Jennie asked.

"No." Jennie turned from the window to look at him. Until now her seatmate hadn't been in a talkative mood. He'd placed his black cowboy hat in the overhead bin, folded his muscular frame into the seat, and fallen asleep. His jeans, cowboy boots, and white western-style shirt suggested he might be a rancher—or a would-be cowboy.

"Then you're in for a real treat." His grin revealed a perfect set of white teeth. "By the way, I'm Marty Danielson."

Jennie returned the smile. "Jennie McGrady."

He tipped his head to one side and fixed his gaze on hers. "You sure got pretty eyes, Jennie McGrady. Deepest blue I've ever seen."

"Thanks." Jennie looked away, feeling a flush rise to her cheeks. "It's . . . um . . . a family trait. My dad and brother . . ." She let her voice trail off. Wanting to change the subject she asked, "Do you live around here?"

"Yep, I'm a freshman at the University of Montana, but I haven't been home in a month. Been on the rodeo circuit. My folks have a little spread south of town." He stretched his long legs, which wasn't easy when you were stuffed into a space that barely fit a ten-year-old. Being fairly tall herself, Jennie could empathize since she'd been sitting in the cramped window seat for the last two hours. She'd worn baggy cotton shorts and a matching shirt, but still felt uncomfortable. Of course, having her right arm in a cast didn't help.

As her gaze drifted to the bright blue fiberglass cast, so did Marty's. "What did you do to your arm?"

Jennie shrugged and gave what had become her standard answer. "Broke it in a fight." In part, her explanation was true. Her arm had taken a blow meant for her head.

When he raised an eyebrow, she grinned and said, "You should see the other guy." Jennie supposed she should be more specific, but how could she tell people she'd been an intended murder victim without spending ages explaining? The cast served as a grim reminder of Jennie's vulnerability, and she didn't like talking about it.

He threw her a look of disbelief, then said, "Must be pretty uncomfortable with your elbow locked like that."

"It's not bad. I'd much rather have it casted bent than straight."

"Broke my arm a couple years ago. A steer threw me, then spun around and stomped on me. Thought I was a goner."

"Sounds dangerous."

His smile faded. "Yep. Life is dangerous." He glanced away briefly then turned back to her, smiling again. "Say . . ." Marty's blue-gray eyes widened. "If you're gonna be in town for a while, maybe you could come by my place for a visit. I'll show you around. Teach you how to rope and ride."

Jennie was flattered, but not all that interested. "I'll be working—I think. My aunt and uncle own a ranch here."

"Yeah? Who are they? I know most of the ranchers in the area."

"Jeff and Maggie White Cloud. Aunt Maggie is my mom's sister. . . ."

Marty's eyes turned cold. "You seem like a nice girl, Jennie, so I'm gonna give you a little advice. When we land, you go to the ticket agent and tell them you want the next flight out of here."

"I don't understand. Why. . . ?"

"Jeff White Cloud and his family's been nothin' but trouble since they showed up out at Dancing Waters less than a year ago. You hang around out there and you're liable to get hurt."

His *advice* surprised her, and she wasn't sure how to respond. "Is that a threat?"

"Nothin' personal. Just that some folks round here aren't too friendly toward Indian lovers."

Jennie ignored the racist remark, hoping he'd answer some of her questions. "Do you know anything about the explosion at their ranch?"

Marty frowned. "Nope. I told you, I've been gone."

"The explosion killed the ranch foreman and injured my uncle—he's still in the hospital."

"Rick Jenkins?" He whistled. "That's too bad. Can't say I'm too surprised though. What does surprise me is that your uncle is still alive." Marty slumped in his seat and stared straight ahead, a frown etching deep lines in his brow. Jennie thought he seemed more shaken by the news than he'd admitted.

As they landed, the prop plane, a thirty-seven-passenger Dornier, bounced a couple of times, then shuddered to a slow roll as the pilot brought it in. Right on time. Twelve-thirty.

Marty retrieved his carry-on, slapped the hat over his ash brown hair, then walked in front of her until they were inside the airport. He was tall—over six feet and the hat and boots gave him even more height. He spun around to face her. The coldness in his eyes had turned to concern. "I meant what I said, Jennie. Jeff White Cloud's got more enemies in the Bitterroot Valley than a killer mountain lion. If you're smart, you'll go back to Portland and forget about helping him."

Marty's warning hadn't exactly scared her, but he had stirred up her interest. Maybe her intuition was onto something after all. She'd suspected foul play from the moment she heard about the so-called accident. Marty could be holding the key to a murder, and Jennie didn't intend to walk away. "Guess I'm not too smart."

Marty gazed at her for a moment, then sighed. "Sorry to hear that." He spun around and walked off.

Jennie watched him go. Excitement shivered through her. At the same time, a band of fear tightened around her throat. *You're not here to solve a mystery, McGrady,* she reminded herself. *You're here to work. And there is nothing to be afraid of—at least not yet.*

Jennie glanced around the terminal, looking for the face she'd memorized from the photo Aunt Maggie had sent. *"Heather will be at the airport to pick you up,"* Maggie had assured her on the phone last night. *"I'll send her in plenty of time to meet your plane."*

Jennie scanned the crowd, but saw no one even resembling the girl in the picture. Heather White Cloud was half

Irish and half Nez Perce Indian. With her coal black hair and wide dark eyes, she looked like a model.

Fifteen minutes later, Jennie slipped on her black leather backpack and scooped up her duffle bag, then headed toward the baggage claim area. Maybe her cousin would be waiting there.

She wasn't.

Jennie retrieved her bags off the conveyer belt, set them on a luggage cart, then settled into a chair near the door where she could watch for Heather. A few minutes later she jumped up and paced, angry one minute and worried the next. Though she fought against it, the conversation she'd had with Marty niggled its way into her guarded thoughts. Jeff White Cloud had enemies. The explosion had killed one man and sent her uncle to the hospital. Could something have happened to Heather, too?

Jennie had Heather paged. No one responded. Another half hour passed and Jennie decided she'd better call the ranch. She groped inside the backpack for her wallet and pulled out Aunt Maggie's letter. She'd located a pay phone and was about to dial the number when she caught a glimpse of her cousin in the baggage claim area.

Jennie started to wave, then stopped. Heather apparently had more important things on her mind than picking up a relative.

She was even more gorgeous in person than in the photograph. Her straight black hair reached the small of her back. A barrette of feathers and a dream catcher adorned one side. Her tan skin contrasted with her gauzy white dress.

A guy in his late teens, maybe early twenties, wearing jeans and a baggy denim shirt stood beside her. Judging by the shoulder bag and camera hanging around his neck, Jennie thought he might be a professional photographer. Shifting his camera aside, he gathered Heather in his arms and kissed her.

Jennie glanced away, but curiosity about the guy and why Heather was with him instead of meeting her made her look back. A few minutes later they separated, and he left the terminal.

Jennie shifted her gaze to Heather. This time Heather spotted her, then smiled and waved. The seventeen-year-old walked toward her, reminding Jennie of a princess, which in a way she was. Her great-grandfather had been a tribal chief. Several people paused to admire her as she passed by. That kind of attention would have mortified Jennie. Heather seemed to enjoy it.

"Hi." Her mouth curved in a perfect smile. "I was afraid I wouldn't recognize you."

Heather's eyes were a deep shade of purple. Jennie could almost see herself in them. She could see something else too. Or maybe she just sensed it. Heather didn't look dangerous, but something about her spelled trouble with a capital T. Jennie thought about taking Marty's advice and flying back home. She wouldn't, of course. Jennie didn't back away from much of anything, especially a mystery.

"I'm sorry I'm late," Heather went on. "But I had a flat on the way in. Can you believe it?"

No. Come on, Heather, tell me the truth. Who was that guy, and why are you lying to me? Jennie wanted to confront her, but didn't. She answered with a polite, "Those things happen." Jennie had a lot of questions but decided to keep her mouth shut for now. After all, even though they were cousins, they had seen each other only once before, at Jennie's dad's funeral.

Fake funeral, Jennie reminded herself. Jason McGrady wasn't really dead, but no one knew that except Jennie, Gram, and a few government officials. He'd been working for the government on a drug case when his plane supposedly went down in the Puget Sound area near Seattle. The authorities never found the plane or his body.

12

A couple of months ago, Jennie discovered the truth. Her father had changed his identity and was working for the Drug Enforcement Agency. But that was another story. Something Jennie tried not to think about too much these days.

Heather nodded toward Jennie's cast. "What happened to your arm?"

"Broke it in a fight."

Heather grimaced. "How awful. You were fighting with someone?"

"Yeah. I didn't start it, but I got in the last lick."

"Oh." Heather stooped to pick up one of Jennie's bags.

Jennie shrugged. So much for making a good impression.

They collected Jennie's luggage and set it at the curb, where Jennie waited while Heather brought around a white Jeep Cherokee.

"Are you hungry?" Heather asked as they left the airport.

"Starved."

"We'll have lunch in town then. I promised Mom I'd run a few errands so we may be a while."

"Sounds good."

They pulled into the Watering Hole Restaurant. The waitress had just seated them when Marty Danielson approached their table.

He folded himself into the seat next to Heather. "Aren't you going to welcome me home?"

Heather ignored him.

The wistful look on Marty's face left no doubt that he didn't dislike all of the White Clouds. Marty switched his gaze to Jennie and flashed her a grin. "I'm sorry if I gave you the wrong impression back at the airport."

"You two know each other?" Heather's dark eyes sent Jennie an off-limits signal, which seemed pretty strange considering Heather's tryst with the photographer.

"Marty!" The harsh voice came from a grim-faced man in a tan shirt and camouflage pants who stood at the cash register. He gave the girls a long disparaging look and motioned for Marty to join him.

"Um—I gotta go." Marty's Adam's apple shifted up and down. His self-assured attitude seemed to melt into the cracks of the rustic wood floor as he stood. "I'll see you."

After the men left, Heather repeated her question.

"He sat next to me on the plane." Jennie shrugged. "So, what's the deal between you two?"

"We dated a few times. Marty's okay, but his dad . . ." Heather dipped her head, but not fast enough to hide the tears pooling in her eyes. "Let's just say he doesn't like half-breeds."

"Marty seems to like you."

"Please don't get involved, Jennie. It doesn't matter anymore. I have other plans."

Plans that no doubt involve the photographer. Jennie picked at her salad, not knowing what to say or if she should say anything at all.

She missed Lisa, her cousin and best friend. They shared everything. Jennie doubted she and Heather would ever be that close. Still, a little comradarie would be nice. A few manners wouldn't hurt either.

Heather spoke little during the rest of their rabbit-food lunch. Jennie had dozens of questions about the ranch, about Aunt Maggie, Uncle Jeff, Heather's twin brother Hazen and their ten-year-old sister, Amber. Heather's mind seemed to be on other matters, so Jennie didn't ask.

A loud voice rose above the normal restaurant din. "No kidding, the buck had antlers on him as wide as this table." She glanced around and had no trouble locating the source. Several men wearing fatigues much like Marty's father occupied a large corner booth in the smoking section. Judging by the noise level and the comment she'd overheard, they were trading hunting stories.

In contrast to the rowdies, two men in business suits sat

in the booth behind Heather. They spoke in hushed voices, using terms like litigation, investments, and loans. When they got up to leave, one of them paused at the table and leveled a concerned gaze at Heather. "Hi, Heather. How's the family?"

Heather shrugged. "Okay, I guess."

"Is your dad home yet? I've been up to the hospital a couple times. I hope he's feeling better."

"He should be home in the next day or two."

"You tell him I asked about him, okay?"

"Sure."

The man nodded and smiled at Jennie, then left without an introduction. Heather turned her attention back to her salad.

Jennie watched out the window as the same two men climbed into a red convertible. They were about the same height but seemed as different as salt and pepper. The one who'd spoken to Heather was light skinned with sandy hair and a broad, friendly smile. The other was more serious looking with olive skin and dark hair.

"Who were those men?" Jennie asked when her curiosity begged for an answer.

Heather glanced out the window and shrugged. "A couple of Dad's friends. The one driving is Alex Dayton. The other one is Greg Bennett. He's Chad Elliot's lawyer."

"Who's Chad Elliot?"

Heather gave her a don't-you-know-anything look and took a sip of water. "He's the guy who's suing us to get his ranch back."

Oh, well, that explains everything. Jennie held back the sarcastic remark. She wanted to find out more, but Heather picked up the bill and slid out of the booth.

After paying the bill and using the rest room, they headed back to the Jeep. Someone had tucked a note under the windshield wiper. Heather ripped it off and threw it to the ground.

"Wait." Jennie retrieved it. "Don't you want to see what it says?"

"No. It won't be any different from the others." Heather climbed into the Jeep and jammed the key into the ignition. "Go ahead. Read it if you . . ." The roar of the engine obliterated the rest of her sentence.

Jennie walked around to the passenger side and unfolded the pale green paper. She closed her eyes and bit her lower lip. No wonder Heather hadn't wanted to read it. Jennie folded the note and stuffed it into the pocket of her shorts.

Even though she'd tucked the words out of sight, they burned in her mind like a searing brand on cowhide.

Tell your daddy next time he won't be so lucky.

2

"Do you know who left the note?" Jennie asked.

"Isn't that obvious? You're the hotshot detective, what do you think?" Heather's disposition had turned even more sour, but this time Jennie didn't blame her. Death threats could do that to a person.

Jennie shrugged. "Marty's dad was in the restaurant. He seemed pretty hostile."

"Him and about a dozen others I could name. It's no use, Jennie. Just forget you saw it."

"Shouldn't we show this note to the police or something?"

Heather sighed. "What's the point? They'd just hand the evidence over to Sheriff Mason, and he'd pretend to check it out."

"Pretend?" Jennie braced herself as Heather made a sharp right turn into the shopping mall parking lot.

"Just forget it. I don't want to talk about it—not now or ever. Do you want to come with me or stay in the car?"

Neither choice appealed to Jennie at the moment, but she opted to go along.

————

"Well, that's it," Heather announced an hour and three stores later as she and Jennie emptied the grocery cart. "We're out of here."

Jennie returned the cart while Heather started the Jeep, and a few minutes later they left the city behind and headed south on Highway 93.

"How far is Dancing Waters?" Jennie asked.

"About sixty-five miles. We're south of Darby, near an even smaller town called Cottonwood. There's a map and a brochure in the glove box if you want to check it out. I don't feel like playing tour guide right now."

Jennie retrieved both and hauled in a deep breath of country air. At least now she could understand her cousin's sullen mood. Getting threats like that had to be terrifying. Still, Jennie wished Heather had more courage. She should be fighting back, not giving up.

"Look," Jennie began. "I know we don't know each other very well, but maybe I can help."

"And just what do you think you could do? Oh, I heard all about how you rescued your little brother and . . . all those other cases. But you have a broken arm and . . . this is different. We're dealing with dangerous people who judge you by the color of your skin. There are too many of them to fight. Daddy should have listened—then maybe Rick wouldn't be dead and Dad wouldn't have lost his leg."

Jennie swallowed hard and closed her eyes. She hadn't known the extent of Jeff's injuries until now and didn't know what to say.

Jennie wished her grandmother could be with her. Gram was one of those people who seemed to know how to deal with everything. Having been a police officer, and now doing occasional jobs for the F.B.I., she had connections all over the country. Besides all that, she wrote articles for several major travel magazines.

Wait! That's it, McGrady. Gram could come to Dancing Waters undercover. She could pretend to be writing an article about the ranch, but in reality she'd be investigating the explosion and the threats.

With her arm still in a cast, Jennie didn't feel safe delving into the case alone, but the thought of Gram coming gave her a renewed sense of power. Jennie made a mental note to call Gram that night, then opened the map and brochure and worked on familiarizing herself with her new environment.

Ranches and companies that built log cabins lined the road. Mountains rose from the valley floor on both sides—the Saffire Mountains to the left and the Selway Bitterroot Wilderness on the right. According to the brochure, Dancing Waters, a working dude ranch, had everything. Guests could relax in natural hot springs, enjoy a massage, eat gourmet meals, or simply enjoy the view.

For the more rugged individual, Dancing Waters offered fishing, white water rafting, backpacking trips into the wilderness, packing with horses and llamas, or mountain climbing. They offered a month-long wilderness experience—where guests hiked into the mountains and lived off the land much as the Indians and the early settlers had.

Jennie leaned forward to place the papers back in the glove box. "Dancing Waters sounds fantastic. Do you guys really do all this stuff?"

"Hmmmph." Heather's enthusiasm was about as high as a gnat's elbow. "We work—the guests have fun—at least that's what they say they're having."

"Sounds as though you don't like it out here."

Heather sneered. "I'm from New York. I love the city. This place bores me. One way or another, I'm getting out."

Okay. Be that way. Jennie slumped back in her seat. So much for having a cousin to pal around with. For the rest of the trip, Jennie watched the scenery—the ranches, and the Bitterroot River as it curved and danced along beside them. *Dancing Waters.* Maybe that's how the ranch got its name. Jennie thought about asking Heather, but didn't—somehow she doubted Heather's answer would do the explanation justice.

At four-thirty Heather turned off the highway and pulled into a long, winding drive. They passed under a black wrought-iron arch with the words "Dancing Waters Dude Ranch" scrolled between double lines. Despite her companion's lack of enthusiasm, Jennie could hardly wait.

They bumped along for another half mile, finally stopping near a complex of at least a dozen buildings.

A little girl ran toward them screaming and ducked for cover behind the Jeep. An ostrich followed a few yards behind. Judging from the fiery look in its eyes, the bird was not a happy camper.

"Oh, great. The ostriches are loose. Poppy's getting away. We'd better head her off before she finds the road. Get in front of her and coax her back to the pen."

"Me?" Jennie sucked in a deep breath hoping a little courage would be mixed with the oxygen. Following Heather's lead, she climbed out of the Jeep and walked toward the huge bird.

"Take it easy, Poppy, you know you're not supposed to be out here," Heather cooed. "Come on, Jennie, hurry. Get over here now."

Jennie quickened her pace and placed herself between the ostrich and the road. The huge bird's long neck shifted up and down, then from one side to the other as if sizing Jennie up. She knew little about ostriches but remembered something about their being strong and powerful.

The girls stretched out their arms to create a human fence. As if sensing the weak link, the six-foot ostrich charged at Jennie.

3

Jennie screamed, then ducked and raised her right arm to protect her head. The ostrich, bent on escape, whacked Jennie's cast with her beak. Poppy sprang back, stunned. She stared vacantly, as though trying to focus her enormous eyes. After a few moments, Poppy turned around and trotted back toward a chain link fence.

"Wow." Heather grinned. "I'm impressed."

Jennie swallowed hard and stared at the shallow dent in her cast. "Me too." She followed Heather past the largest of the buildings into a courtyard. At the far end of the compound, three ostriches skittered back and forth, obviously trying to break free.

Dozens of people in a variety of shapes and sizes had gathered to watch the commotion. Several of the braver souls formed a semicircle around the loose ostriches, waving their hands and trying to herd the creatures back through the open gate. Three long-necked creatures loped along the perimeter of the human fence, scanning their captors, probably looking for an easy way out. Jennie joined the circle, but held her cast at the ready—just in case. One by one the birds gave up their quest and returned to the pen.

Before Jennie could recover, a woman with freckled skin and kinky auburn hair moved in close beside her. She wore a long denim skirt and vest, and a cream-colored cotton shirt with *Dancing Waters Dude Ranch* embroidered on the pocket. "Jennie, it's so good to have you here."

"I'm glad to be here—I think." Jennie wrapped her arms around her aunt, careful not to whack her with the cast. Maggie was seven years older than Mom, a couple inches taller, and thinner than Jennie remembered.

After a thorough hug, Aunt Maggie let her go. "What a welcome for you. Sorry about Poppy. She's usually not that aggressive." Maggie nodded toward the ostrich pen. "They may be worth a lot of money, but sometimes I wonder if they're worth the trouble."

She glanced down at Jennie's cast and frowned. "Good thing it was the cast and not your flesh. These guys may look harmless, but they can be mean. Some of them are ten feet tall and there's no stopping them once they decide to run. Fortunately, the girls in this pen are fairly docile."

"That's docile?"

Maggie examined Jennie's cast again. "Does your arm hurt?"

"Not anymore." Jennie glanced back at the pen. "Do the ostriches get out often?"

Maggie shook her head and sighed. "Someone must have left the gate unlatched. Probably Amber."

"I heard that, Mother, and you are wrong, wrong, wrong! I shut the gate tight and checked it." A lanky young girl with red-gold hair several shades lighter than Maggie's seemed on the verge of tears. "Someone else did it. Probably on purpose, like all the other stuff."

"We'll talk about it later, honey." Maggie gathered her close and stroked her curls. "We have a guest."

"Hi." She peered up at Jennie as she tucked her hands in the back pockets of her jeans. "Are you my cousin?"

"That depends. Are you Amber?"

Amber nodded and looked at her mother. "I thought you said there'd be three of them."

22

Maggie chuckled. "There will be. Eventually." To Jennie she said, "Your mom called earlier."

"When is she coming? Did she get the okay to bring Hannah?" The McGradys had been caring for Hannah, their four-year-old neighbor, in the weeks following her kidnapping. Unfortunately they'd hit a snag in taking her across state lines. Mom and Nick, Jennie's five-year-old brother, stayed behind to work things out with Children's Services. Since Maggie had been desperate for help, Mom insisted Jennie go on ahead.

"Um . . . They've run into some trouble, but you're not to worry. They should be here in three or four days."

"Three or four days!" Amber rolled her eyes. "I was planning on giving them a tour."

"Will I do?" Jennie asked. "I could use a guide. This place is huge."

"That's a wonderful idea, Amber," Maggie said, "but first we need to concentrate on dinner." To Jennie she said, "This is the height of the tourist season and I have a hundred guests looking forward to meal time. I still have to prepare the ostrich."

Jennie's mouth dropped open. "You eat them?"

"Occasionally. They're expensive, but . . ." Maggie closed her eyes in an expression of ecstasy. "Unbelievably good."

"Get used to it, Jennie," Amber advised. "This is the farm. We raise animals to eat." She took a deep breath. "That's what Daddy says. Actually, I'm thinking seriously about becoming a vegetarian."

Maggie's eyes sparkled with hidden laughter as she winked at Jennie. "I'll remember that next time we have a barbeque." She hugged Amber close, then released her. "Enough talk for now. We've got work to do. Amber, honey, get one of the hands to bring Jennie's things up to the house. Jennie, you can go on up to the house now if you want. Or if you'd rather you can just wander around here, maybe find a comfy place to rest. We'll have some time to chat later."

"I'm not much for sitting around—can I do something to help?"

Maggie glanced at the cast. "I certainly could use an extra hand in the dining room, but are you sure you can bus tables with that cast?"

"Sure. The doctor said I can do almost anything except straighten my arm." She held up her left hand. "Besides, I'm getting pretty good at being a lefty."

Maggie didn't look convinced. "Okay, if you're sure. But if you get tired or start hurting, I want you to stop."

Jennie agreed.

"Before you start working, why don't you take a few minutes to freshen up in one of the bathrooms here in the lodge?" Maggie sighed and hugged her again. "I know this isn't much of a welcome, but we'll catch up later. I promise."

Maggie escorted Jennie into an enormous log structure. Inside the lodge, rough-hewn timbers stretched across the rafters. A dozen or so guests sat in the plush leather couches and chairs in the lobby. A gray stone fireplace took up an entire wall, separating the lobby from a large dining hall. A few guests were already seated at round tables covered with white linen cloths. The dining room extended to a large outside deck overlooking a river. A small gift shop occupied one corner.

Maggie showed her the kitchen, then left her inside the rest room. Jennie would have loved a twenty-minute shower, but settled instead on washing her hands and face. She looked fairly good for someone who'd come five-hundred miles, been threatened by a cowboy, lied to by a cousin, and done battle with an ostrich.

Before heading back to the kitchen, she took a moment to call home. When no one answered, Jennie left a message on the machine and hung up. She tried calling Gram, but got the answering machine there as well. "God, please let everything go okay with Hannah," Jennie whispered as she glanced upward and walked through the milling guests toward the kitchen.

Helping with the meal turned out to be much more interesting than Jennie had imagined. She bussed tables, served food, talked to guests and, from time to time, paused to enjoy the view of the river as it passed—no, danced—beside the deck. *Dancing Waters*. That had to be how the ranch got its name.

At seven-thirty the last guest wandered out of the dining room. She'd heard nothing but praises about the food and could hardly wait for the meal Maggie had promised. Jennie picked up the dishes and silverware and carried the tray into the kitchen.

"Great job, Jennie." Maggie squeezed her shoulders. "Now it's our turn. Come on. We'll eat on the deck." Maggie led the way, and within minutes Jennie was drooling over the salad, steak, wild rice, and baby asparagus spears.

Maggie waited for Heather and Amber to join them, then said grace. Famished, Jennie cut into her steak and took a bite. "Mmmm." She raised her head only to discover three pairs of eyes trained on her.

"Um . . . did I do something wrong?"

"Not at all, Jennie." Maggie grinned. "Do you like the meat?"

"Yes. This is the best steak I've ever eaten." She sliced off another bite and lifted the fork to her mouth.

Amber giggled. "It's ostrich."

Jennie closed her mouth and set the fork back down. "No way. This is red meat—it's a steak. An ostrich is a bird. Wouldn't it taste more like chicken?"

"Nope. That's ostrich," Amber said. "We knew you wouldn't try it if we told you."

"You're right about that." Jennie took another bite. "This is so good."

"Wow, Jennie likes it. . . ." Heather speared a lettuce leaf. Her voice dripped with sarcasm and Jennie wondered what she'd done to make her cousin angry.

"Heather, please." Maggie placed a hand on her daughter's arm. "Not now."

"Jennie already knows how much I hate this place. Why pretend we're all one big happy family when we're not?"

"Couldn't you at least make an effort?"

"I am, Mother. You haven't given me much choice." Heather pushed her chair back and left the table.

After dinner Maggie, Amber, and Jennie walked up the hill to where the family lived. Unlike the rustic log cabins and lodge, the White Cloud home was as elegant as a Victorian mansion.

"You'll be sharing a room with Heather," Maggie said as they stepped into the tiled entry. "I hope that will be okay for you. Heather isn't usually this . . . ah . . . negative."

Amber rolled her eyes and took hold of Jennie's hand. "She has been since we moved out here. Come on, I'll show you where your room is. If my sister gets too weird, you can move in with me."

"I'll keep that in mind." Jennie wished some of Amber's charm would rub off on Heather.

She followed the ten-year-old up the winding staircase and down a long hall. "This one is Heather's." Amber pointed to the bedroom on the left. "And the bathroom." Amber pushed open the door to reveal a large room with a claw-foot tub. "The next one is the guest room. Your mom's gonna sleep there when she comes. Mom and Dad have the one at the end of the hall and my room is next to them." Amber skipped a door. It must have been her brother's. Jennie wondered why she didn't mention it.

Tour completed, they entered Heather's bedroom.

Heather wasn't there, and that suited Jennie fine. A large white bear, similar to one of hers, rested against a pink ruffled pillow. His whimsical black button eyes almost made her feel at home.

The room had two beds, and since her luggage had been set in front of the one on the left, Jennie assumed she'd be sleeping there.

"You can put your stuff in here," Amber said as she opened the door to a walk-in closet.

A poster of Heather and Hazen in native American costumes hung over a white chest of drawers. "Amber, where's your brother?"

Amber clasped her hands in front of her and gazed at the picture. Moisture pooled in her deep golden eyes. "Gone. He went away after my dad got hurt."

"Just like that? And you don't know where he is?"

"Nope. He just disappeared."

"Did someone kidnap him or. . . ?"

"I don't think so. He was with Daddy and Rick—that's the foreman that got killed. Hazen drove Daddy to the hospital, and we haven't seen him since."

Jennie shook her head. Maybe she had a misplaced sense of responsibility, but it seemed to her that Heather and Hazen should be helping their folks instead of feeling sorry for themselves. In her family if anyone got hurt, the others all pitched in to help. They didn't run away. *It isn't any of your business, McGrady. And don't be so judgmental—you've only been here a few hours. If Amber's story is right, Hazen may have saved his father's life.*

"Amber," Maggie called. "You need to get ready for bed."

Amber rolled her eyes. "I never get to stay up late." After saying good-night and giving Jennie a hug, Amber left.

Jennie began emptying her suitcase. Every time she passed the twin's poster she stopped to examine it. Something about it—about them—drew her like an invisible thread. She felt connected, yet distant. What a mystery they were. Beautiful, yet dangerous.

Dangerous? Oh, come on, McGrady. So Heather met a guy at the airport, then lied to you about it. And Hazen left home after the explosion. That doesn't make them dangerous. You're letting your imagination go wild again.

She continued to stare at the picture. Yet there was something. She'd seen it earlier in Heather. Now she saw the same expression on Hazen's handsome face—in those haunting dark eyes.

Jennie shook her head to dispel her foolish thoughts, then finished unpacking and hurried downstairs.

She found Maggie in the front room relaxing in a rocking chair. With her shoes off and her thick red hair cascading around her shoulders, she resembled Mom even more than before.

Jennie felt sad for her. She'd been through so much with her husband hurt and in the hospital. Why did Heather and Hazen have to be so selfish? Jennie closed out the angry thoughts and gave her aunt a hug.

"Did you get settled in?" Maggie asked.

"Yep. I love the room. And the house."

"I love it too. The original owners had it built in the early 1900s." She smiled. "Would you believe they ordered it out of a Sears & Roebuck catalog?"

Jennie sank into a couch next to Maggie's chair. "Really?"

"Really. In those days you could order anything. It's solid too. Better than most of the houses built today. All we had to do was resurface the flooring in a few of the rooms and paint."

Jennie wiggled deeper into the plush cushioned couch and closed her eyes.

She felt something on her arm and jumped. "Sorry if I startled you, Jennie." Maggie smiled down at her. "You look like you're about to fall asleep."

At Maggie's suggestion, Jennie went upstairs and crawled into bed.

Some time later, a door clicked shut, pulling Jennie out of a sound sleep. Heather turned on a multicolored stained-glass lamp beside her bed, flooding the room in rainbows.

"I'm sorry," Heather said when Jennie sat up. "I didn't mean to wake you."

Jennie yawned. "What time is it?"

"Just nine-thirty."

Jennie had slept for only twenty minutes, but the short nap had revived her.

"Listen, Jennie. I've been acting like a brat, and I hope you'll forgive me. My only excuse is that so much has been happening around here lately. None of this is your fault and . . ."

"Hey, it's okay. I understand."

Heather smiled. "I'm glad. We kind of started off on the wrong foot, didn't we?"

Even though Heather's icy antagonism seemed to be melting, Jennie didn't trust her. "I'm willing to start over if you are."

"Great." Heather opened her closet door and stepped inside saying she needed to change. Jennie expected to see her in pajamas, but Heather emerged wearing a pair of black jeans and a loose white blouse under a black leather vest. A silver and turquoise necklace hung around her slender neck.

"You're going out?" Jennie asked.

"I have to meet someone." She shrugged on a black suede jacket. "I know it's asking a lot, but this is important to me."

"And you don't want me to tell your mom?" Jennie bit the inside of her cheek.

Heather winced. "I wouldn't ask, but Mom has so much on her mind with Dad being gone and Hazen running off. I don't want her to worry."

Jennie tossed her covers aside. "Are you doing something she'd be worried about?"

"No, of course not."

"Let me come with you."

"No! Stay out of this, Jennie. The less you know the better." Heather opened her bedroom window then disappeared in the foliage of a large maple tree. Jennie pulled her clothes on and stuffed her feet into her tennis shoes. By the time Jennie stepped onto the roof, Heather had reached the fence at the edge of the lawn. Jennie eyed the giant tree, then her casted arm, and took a deep breath. Using her left hand to grasp the limbs and her right arm for balance, she stepped onto an ample branch next to the roof and began her descent. Fortunately, the tree had been made for climbing and Jennie had no problem jumping from the lowest branch, which hung only three feet from the ground.

Once on the ground, Jennie glanced off in the direction she'd last seen her cousin. With the flashlight marking the way, Heather was heading into the woods.

A full moon illuminated the path. In the distance the beam from Heather's flashlight bounced through the trees. Jennie slowed and followed a safe distance behind.

"Who's there?" Heather stopped and spun around.

Jennie ducked behind a fir tree and waited for Heather to move on. Maintaining a greater distance between them, she trailed Heather for what seemed like forever, then stopped when the beam from the flashlight vanished. She strained to hear her cousin's footfall but heard only the sound of chattering leaves as a cool breeze swept through the forest.

Jennie hugged herself to ward off the chill. Was Heather playing games? "Okay, Heather, you win. I'm going back now."

No one answered. A twig snapped. She spun around in the direction of the sound. "Heather?"

Jennie cowered in the chilling silence. *This is ridiculous,*

McGrady. Go back to the house. She took a step in the direction she thought she'd come. The moon still provided a scant, filtered light, but nothing looked familiar.

A coyote howled. Then another. Jennie wrapped her jacket tightly around her. A cloud drifted across the moon, plunging the forest into total darkness.

4

"Okay," she whispered. "Just keep calm. There's a way out. You just have to find it." Jennie took several deep breaths and willed the fear to subside. She'd been in worse situations.

The oxygen revived her and cleared her mind. She sat on a stump and looked up at the sliver of light that lined the cloud. It seemed to promise hope and a way out. Jennie prayed for wisdom and courage. "And God," she added. "If you could spare a guardian angel, I could use one about now."

The leaves rustled again. For a moment she blamed it on the wind but felt no breeze against her skin. She swallowed hard. *There's no need to panic, McGrady. It could be anything. An owl, a squirrel, a racoon* . . . Jennie stopped her imagination from coming up with anything bigger.

The moon peeked out from behind the cloud. She tried to remember where it had been earlier, but couldn't. Jennie shivered and buttoned up her denim jacket, wishing she'd grabbed a sweatshirt.

She jumped up and marched in a circle, hoping the movement would warm her. Jennie thought about lying down and trying to sleep. Morning would bring the sun and she could use it as a guide. No, she did not want to spend the night in these woods. It was too cold and there were wild animals—mountain lions and bears. There had to be another option.

32

Heading northeast would take her to the east fork of the Bitterroot River. "The river!" Jennie stopped pacing. "It flows right through the ranch. If I can find it, I can follow it back." But how? She had no idea which direction she should go.

Leaves rustled again.

"Be still, my child." A deep masculine voice resonated through the forest. "Listen to the earth."

Jennie sucked in a wild breath and whipped around. "Who's there?" She saw no one and heard only the sounds of the trees. *There's got to be an explanation*, Jennie told herself. *Maybe it was God, or that angel you asked for. Or maybe it was just your imagination.*

Jennie pressed back against a tree and willed her racing heart to slow down. *Be still*, the voice had said. She remembered a story she'd heard in Sunday school about a prophet, Elijah. He'd been in the wilderness. God had told him to be still. Was God sending her the same message?

Listen to the earth. Jennie sat on the stump again and tried to clear her mind of everything except the sounds around her.

Being from the Northwest, Jennie knew the sound of water rushing over rocks. She'd even fallen over a waterfall once. If she could hear the river and follow the sound, maybe . . .

Somewhere in the distance an owl hooted. She concentrated harder and thought she could hear a steady shushing sound. Leaves in the wind? Or dancing waters? She couldn't be sure.

Listen to the earth. Of course. Jennie scrunched down on the forest floor. She'd seen movies where Indian guides would press their ears to the ground in order to hear the sound of horses' hooves. They could even tell what direction the riders were coming from.

Jennie put a hand over her left ear and pressed her right to the ground. "I can hear it," she said after a few minutes.

Excitement bubbled like a spring inside her. "I can really hear the water."

She walked in a widening circle, stopping to listen at intervals to determine which direction she should go. She paused where she heard the rushing sound the loudest, then set out to find the river she hoped would take her back to the ranch. Jennie prayed she was heading toward the right river and in the right direction.

As she walked, the sound of the water grew stronger. After about ten minutes, the forest gave way to a pasture and the distant lights told her she wasn't far from the highway. She stopped a moment at the edge of the forest and sat on a fallen log to rest. She could see the river now. Moonbeams turned the swirling waters from gray to silver, giving it a magical look. "Thank you," she called in case the owner of the voice was listening.

"You're welcome."

Jennie stopped and whipped around, half expecting to see an angel. But no one was there. Had she really heard the voice again? Had it been an angel? Or God—or merely the wind?

A cool breeze lifted the loosened tendrils of hair from Jennie's cheeks. With the moon still lighting her way, she broke into a run.

By the time Jennie reached the house, it had started to rain. She shuddered, partly from the cold and partly from the knowledge that if she hadn't listened to the voice, she'd still be wandering around out there.

Jennie climbed up the tree and onto the roof near Heather's bedroom window. She tried to push it up. When it wouldn't budge, she tapped on the glass. After several minutes Heather peered out, a confused expression on her face. Finally she unlatched the window and slid it open. "What are you doing out there?" she whispered.

"As if you didn't know. Why did you leave me alone in the woods?"

"I don't know what you're talking about. I didn't even know you went out." Heather straightened. "You followed me?"

"I . . . I was worried about you."

"You didn't need to be. I can take care of myself."

"So I see." Jennie had more questions for Heather, such as: Why did you lock the window? Didn't you think I'd make it back? Did you lose me out there on purpose? But Jennie didn't ask them. Instead she changed into her nightgown and crawled into bed.

Sleep didn't come easily. *Dangerous.* The word wove itself over, around, and through recent memories of being lost in the woods and being left at the airport. Marty and his dad. The photographer. The poster of Hazen and Heather. The explosion. Together they wove a dark and haunting tapestry. Did Heather know more than she was letting on? She wanted to go back to New York, but surely not badly enough to . . . No. Heather would never do anything to hurt her father—or would she?

———

The twangy sounds of country music drifted into Jennie's foggy brain, then stopped. She opened one eye expecting to see the large red numbers of her alarm announcing the time. It wasn't there. Neither was her nightstand. Then she remembered. She rubbed her eyes and sat up. A light went on in the walk-in closet. Outside, the sky glowed with the first blush of dawn. The neon green hands on Heather's clock radio read five-thirty. Was her cousin sneaking out again?

A few minutes later, Heather snapped off the closet light and emerged wearing a pink T-shirt imprinted with a Dancing Waters logo and black jeans. "Sorry if I woke you. I tried to be quiet."

"It's okay. What are you doing up so early?"

Heather flipped on the overhead light. "I ask myself that every morning. You'd better get used to it. We start work between six and six-thirty." Heather covered her shirt with a fringed black suede jacket, then pulled on her leather boots.

Jennie moaned. "So what kind of work do you do?"

"Different things. Today I'm taking a group of executives on a one-day trail ride." Heather ran a brush through her hair, separated it into three strands, and began braiding.

"Sounds like fun. Maybe I could go along sometime."

"Maybe." Heather secured the long braid with a band, then picked up a barrette and attached it in the back where the braid began. From it hung a white feather with a pink tip and a dream catcher.

Jennie had noticed about a dozen or so feathered clips in various colors hanging in the closet the night before. "You have a lot of those."

"Feel free to wear one if you want. I like them. Eric says they . . ." Heather's gaze met Jennie's in the mirror. "Don't ask." She said good-bye and left.

Jennie thought about going back to sleep, but her mind was already up and running, so she joined it. Wrapping her cast in plastic to keep it dry, she showered, then dressed, and hurriedly brushed through her hair. After making three attempts to pull her thick mane into a ponytail, she gave up. The cast made some things impossible. Maybe she could ask Maggie to put her hair up later. She tossed the brush on the dresser and headed downstairs.

Heather pushed her chair back just as Jennie sat down. "Don't worry, Mom. I can handle it. Besides, you know Papa will be out there. Sometimes I think he's more spirit than human the way he looks out for us. I'll be back around five."

More spirit than human? Jennie thought about the voice she'd heard the night before.

"Pass the syrup, please." Amber stuck her hand toward

Maggie and accepted the bottle.

"Did you sleep well, Jennie?" Maggie asked.

"I had a little trouble at first, but . . ." She glanced at Heather who shot her a don't-tell warning before heading out the door. "I did okay."

Jennie speared a slice of French toast and grabbed a couple pieces of bacon off the tray as Maggie passed it to her. "Who was Heather talking about?"

"Our grandfather, Joseph." Amber supplied the information. "Papa knows everything. But he isn't the spirit Heather was talking about. She thinks it is, but it's really White Cloud—our great-grandfather. He died in 1972 but his spirit . . ."

"Amber," Maggie rested a hand on Amber's arm. "What did I tell you about repeating those stories?" She winked at Jennie. "I don't know where she gets some of these ideas. She has such a vivid imagination. I can assure you, we have no ghosts, and Joseph is very human and very normal. You'll meet him soon."

Amber bounced up and down. "I'll take you to his house. Can I, Mom?"

"Not today. Maybe tomorrow. I need Jennie to work today." She gave Jennie an apologetic look. "That is, if you're up to it."

"Sure. Do you want me to help in the dining room again?"

Maggie picked up her coffee and scanned the clipboard lying beside her plate. "I've got a full crew in the kitchen. But I could use some help in maid service. Two of my girls called in sick. If it's okay with you, I'll rotate you around to different jobs. It will give you a chance to familiarize yourself with the ranch and to meet the staff."

"That sounds great." Even though Maggie hadn't said so, Jennie got the impression her aunt wanted her to keep an eye out for signs of trouble. Did she suspect disloyalty among staff members?

The back door opened and closed. Maggie glanced toward the kitchen. "That must be Bob." Turning to Jennie she explained, "Bob Lopez is the ranch manager—been here since Jeff was a little boy."

"Mornin', Maggie." Bob Lopez plucked off his beige cowboy hat and set it on the credenza, then sauntered toward them. He lowered his short, thick body onto the vacant chair between Amber and Maggie and ruffled Amber's hair with a large, calloused hand. "How's my little leprechaun?"

Amber giggled. "I'm not a leprechaun."

He reached for the carafe of coffee and poured himself a cup. "Then you must be my lucky charm." His dark brown eyes twinkled as he spoke, then clouded when he turned back to Maggie.

"Uh oh, I know that look," Maggie said. "More trouble?"

"'Fraid so." He took a tentative sip of the hot brew. "Danielson called this morning. Somebody cut the fencing again. Says there's about a dozen head of our buffalo in with his prize steers. He's afraid they'll contaminate his herd."

"Our buffalo are clean. Did you tell him that?"

"Yep. He's still threatening to sue."

Maggie slapped her cup down on the table. Coffee slopped out onto the bright floral tablecloth. She didn't bother mopping it up. "I'll bet anything he cut the wire himself." She looked at Jennie. "Another in a long string of irritations. They're all aimed at forcing us to sell."

"This your niece?" Lopez asked.

"Oh . . . ah . . . yes." Maggie paused for introductions, then added, "Jennie'll be helping out wherever we need her."

Lopez leaned back in the chair and winked at Jennie. "I could use another hand repairing that fence."

Maggie shook her head. "Not yet. I'm not sure Jennie's even ridden a horse."

"Only on the merry-go-round," Jennie admitted, "but I'd love to try. I've always wanted to ride." Along with mysteries, some of Jennie's favorite books were about horses. Lately she'd been reading a series by Lauraine Snelling. If imagination counted, she'd ridden at least a hundred times.

"I love your enthusiasm, Jennie, and we'll make sure you get your share of riding, but it's not safe right now. We've had some poachers and . . ." She hesitated and closed her eyes.

"Maggie's right. I wasn't thinking. We'll be working close to where the truck exploded."

"Bob, please. Jennie doesn't need to hear this." Maggie's hands shook as she grasped the table and pushed herself back. "Take a couple of the men out to help you. And be careful."

"Yes'm." Lopez took a gulp of his coffee and retrieved his hat.

"Oh, and, Bob—" Maggie stopped him on her way to put dishes in the sink. She'd lowered her voice, but Jennie overheard. "I know Jeff would disagree, but maybe you'd better start carrying your rifles out there—just in case."

5

"This is the last cabin, Jennie." Heidi Copeland, the maid service supervisor, adjusted the pillows on her side of the bed and waited for Jennie to do the same. "Are you ready to quit for the day?" She blew her wispy flaxen bangs off her forehead.

"I am definitely ready," Jennie said, "but I should check with Aunt Maggie. She might need me to help somewhere else."

"Such dedication for one so young." Deep dimples appeared on Heidi's flushed cheeks. "Maggie and Jeff are lucky to have you." She reached around to her back and tucked a loose end of her aqua Dancing Waters T-shirt into her jeans.

Nearly all the staff wore jeans and shirts with a Dancing Waters logo, and Jennie was no exception. It was a uniform of sorts, only they could choose whatever color they wanted. Jennie had picked a royal blue to match her cast.

"Thanks. I could say the same thing about you. You always seem so happy."

"I am happy, Jennie. Oh, sometimes I miss my family in Switzerland, but this is my home now."

"I'm curious, how did you end up in Montana?"

"I came to see the big sky and I fell in love with the land and its people."

One person especially, Jennie noted. Heidi's face took on

a special glow when she talked about John, her husband of three months. She and John had been working at Dancing Waters for a year—since Maggie and Jeff had opened it as a dude ranch.

Heidi supervised maid service. John worked as a ranch hand under Bob Lopez.

Jennie straightened and rubbed her back. It had been a grueling day. Since breakfast, Jennie had been introduced to more people than she could count. Okay, maybe she was exaggerating, but between guests and staff members she'd met at least fifty. She just hoped they wouldn't expect her to remember their names.

"Do you live here on the ranch?" Jennie asked as they left the cabin area and walked toward the main lodge.

"We did before we got married. The staff lodging is in the dorms behind the cabins. Jeff and Maggie offered to let us use one of the guest cabins, but they are much too small. We have a home in Cottonwood."

"Heidi," Jennie hesitated. She'd been wanting to ask the question all day, but the time hadn't seemed right. "I know there's been a lot of problems at the ranch, and I wondered if you had any ideas about it."

"Ideas? I don't understand."

"Do you know who might want them to leave?"

"No." The dimples vanished. Deep worry lines appeared on her forehead. "It would be best if you didn't ask such questions, Jennie. It is dangerous to know too much about these things."

"What about this Chad Elliot guy? Heather says he's suing."

Heidi shook her head. "I'm sorry, Jennie. I know nothing of Mr. Elliot—only rumors that he is an angry man."

They climbed the steps to the lodge. Instead of going in the main entrance, they followed the porch around to a side door marked "Office." Jennie collided with a young man backing out.

"I'm sorry," he said, turning around. "I should have been watching." He raked a hand through his walnut brown hair and smiled.

What are you doing here? Jennie started to ask, then caught herself. He was the guy she'd seen at the airport with Heather. And she wasn't supposed to know him.

Maggie joined them in the doorway. "Eric, this is my niece Jennie and this is Heidi. Heidi supervises our maid service. Ladies, meet Eric Summers. He's a photographer and has offered to do some promotional work for me. He'll also be helping Bob with maintenance around the ranch.

So this was Eric. Heather had let his name slip that morning. Jennie had a zillion questions.

"I was about to take Eric to the men's quarters. Did you two want to talk to me?"

"Yes," Heidi said, "but I can wait."

"Why don't I take him over, Aunt Maggie? It'll save you some time." *And give me a chance to check him out.*

"That'll be great." Maggie gave Jennie a knowing wink. "Eric, why don't you get settled? I'll have one of the men show you around after dinner and we'll talk in the morning. I should have a schedule ready for you by then."

"Sure thing, Mrs. White Cloud. And thanks." He turned to Heidi before leaving. "Nice meeting you." Eric's gaze lingered on the Swiss Miss a little longer than necessary.

"You can stop drooling, Eric," Jennie said when they were out of earshot. "She's married."

"Who?" He tossed her a questioning look.

Jennie shook her head. "You really are a piece of work. I don't know what Heather sees in you."

He stopped and grabbed her arm. "Heather . . . you know?"

"Of course I know." Jennie shook off his hand. She didn't

bother to tell him she knew very little, and hoped he wouldn't guess. "I'm her cousin. We share a room together. I was there when she snuck out of her room last night to meet you."

He frowned. "She said she wasn't going to tell anyone."

Bingo. She'd guessed right. "Well, don't blame her. I saw you two at the airport yesterday."

His tan cheeks turned a ruddy rose. "Um, look, Jennie. I'd appreciate it if you didn't say anything to Heather about . . ." He glanced back at the lodge. "I didn't mean anything by it."

"You mean Heidi?"

"Yeah. Heather and I go back a long way. We went to the same school."

"In New York."

He nodded. "We had a good thing going. She's a terrific model. I've already won some awards for my photography. I'd started putting together a portfolio and we had an agent ready to take us on."

"Hmm. You must have been really upset when her parents decided to move out west. She told me how much she hates it out here."

"You might find this hard to believe, but I love Heather. And one way or another we'll find a way to be together."

One way or another. While Jennie couldn't imagine Heather deliberately hurting her dad, she had no trouble adding Eric to her suspect list. His motive could be love, but Jennie suspected the stronger motive was money. If Heather made it in the modeling industry, she could be worth millions.

There's just one problem, McGrady. He wasn't here. He couldn't have had anything to do with the explosion—unless . . . "Is this your first trip to Montana?"

He nodded. "It's taken me a while to raise enough money."

They reached the bunk houses and Jennie stopped. End

of trail on both counts. Eric thanked her and said he'd see her later.

Jennie ambled back to the main lodge. Now what? She hated being stuck in the middle. So what had she done? Wedged herself in even deeper. Heather was headed for trouble, and Jennie didn't know what to do about it. Should she tell Maggie and risk alienating her cousin forever? Jennie rubbed her forehead. No, she'd confront Heather first and try to convince her to stop sneaking around and to tell her parents about Eric and her dreams to be a model. Maybe they could compromise.

Jennie knew what it was like to deal with a parent who didn't approve of her kid's career choice. Mom didn't want Jennie to go into law enforcement, but she was beginning to soften.

Amber hopped down the steps as Jennie approached. "There you are," she said in an accusing voice. "I've been waiting to show you around."

Jennie eyed the black, gold-trimmed Dodge Caravan that sat in the driveway. "Who's here?

Amber wrinkled her nose. "Mr. Bennett. He's talking to Mom."

Jennie took a step up, battling against the urge to sneak up to the door and eavesdrop. When the office door opened she jumped back.

"I hope when the litigation is all over you and Jeff will be able to overlook our differences. We should get together for dinner in town." Bennett extended a hand to Maggie and she shook it. "I hope so too, Greg. Tell Melissa I said hi."

"I surely will." He nodded at Jennie and Amber as he descended the stairs and stepped into his van. "I'll stop out again when Jeff is home. You have him call me, okay? There's still a chance we can settle out of court. I'm trying to talk my client into a compromise." He shrugged and offered an apologetic half smile.

Jennie wanted to sit down with her aunt and learn more about Bennett and his client, Chad Elliot, but Maggie had other plans.

"Oh good," she said, turning her attention from Bennett to Amber. "I see you've found her. Jennie, this would be a good time to take that tour with Amber. She wants to introduce you to some of our four-legged guests." The phone rang and Maggie excused herself, then hurried in to answer it.

Jennie thought about waiting around for a few minutes so she could ask Maggie some questions about the land deal. Like, if Bennett and Jeff were friends, why would he take Elliot's case? As she thought about it, Jennie realized it wasn't all that unusual. Lawyers often defended people they didn't necessarily agree with.

"Come on, Jen. What are you waiting for?"

"I'd like to talk to your mom for a minute."

"You might have a long wait." Amber sighed and pointed to the red convertible pulling up to the lodge.

Alex Dayton stepped out of the car and waved. He'd exchanged his Brooks Brothers' suit for khaki slacks and a brick-red shirt. "Hey Amber." He came along beside them and ruffled Amber's hair. "How's it going, Sunshine?"

"Fine."

"Your mother in the office?"

"Yep."

He reached into his shirt pocket and pulled out a Snicker's bar and handed it to Amber, gave Jennie a quick nod, then ran up the steps and disappeared into the office.

"See, I told you she was too busy." Amber yanked on Jennie's hand again, and this time she gave in and followed. Over the next hour, Amber introduced Jennie to two dogs, three cats, a shaggy new llama named Socks and his mother, Angel, named, Jennie suspected, for her tender disposition, her white coat, and her beautiful sky-blue eyes. Now it was time to meet Gabby.

"Gabby will be your horse while you're here." Amber led the way through the largest horse barn Jennie had ever seen. "He's a six-year-old gelding. He loves people and talks all the time. Come on, I'll show you." Amber approached a white horse and patted his nose. "Hi, Gabby." The horse snuffled a greeting and nodded. "I want you to meet my cousin Jennie."

"Nice to meet you, Jennie." A gravelly male voice said.

Jennie jumped back, thinking for a moment the horse had spoken. She laughed when she spotted the buckskin-colored hat. "You had me going there for a minute."

A short man in his late fifties unlatched the stable door and stepped out. He had the weathered look of a rancher who'd spent too many summers in the sun. His bright blue eyes twinkled as they caught Jennie's questioning gaze.

Amber took Jennie's hand and pulled her forward. "This is Dusty Coburn. He runs the stables."

"Howdy there, Jennie. Amber tells me you want to learn how to ride. Well, you've come to the right place." He lifted his hat and wiped perspiration from his brow with a red handkerchief he'd pulled from his back pocket. "You hang around awhile, get to know old Gabby here and we'll get 'im saddled up for ya."

Dusty limped away and disappeared into an office at the far end of the barn. "He's got arthritis," Amber said before Jennie could ask. "Dad says it's from all those falls he took when he was a jockey."

"Does he still ride?"

"Every day. Come on—you gotta meet the real Gabby."

Jennie reached up to stroke Gabby's white forelock, then yanked her hand back when the horse whinnied and shook his head. "I don't think he likes me."

"Oh, sure he does. Let's get him some grain and a few carrots and you'll be his friend for life."

Jennie spent the next half hour getting acquainted with

Gabby and several of the other horses including Cinnamon, Amber's mare. Amber worked with her on grooming skills until Dusty arrived to give Jennie her first riding lesson.

Following Dusty's instructions, Jennie led Gabby into the arena behind the stable. She watched as Dusty cupped his hands to give Amber a hand up onto Cinnamon's back.

Jennie raised her casted right arm up and rested it on the saddle. She slipped her foot into the stirrup, then grabbed the saddle horn with her left hand to steady herself, bounced up, and swung her right leg over the saddle.

"Hoowee," Dusty hooted. "You sure you've never been on a horse before, Jennie? You're a natural."

Jennie shrugged. "Not unless you count carousels."

He chuckled. "Who'd a thought it?"

"I just hope the cast won't be a problem."

Dusty shook his head. "Naw—you'll be holding the reins and guiding him with your left hand. You should do just fine."

For the next hour, Dusty taught her how to handle the reins to guide Gabby through the various courses he'd set up in the riding arena. They circled the arena dozens of times as she practiced turning and backing up, walking and trotting. Jennie loved it. Of course she'd always known she would.

That night, Jennie helped bus tables again and, after a late supper, dragged herself up to bed. A scraping sound woke her as Heather crawled in through the window. Jennie glanced at the clock. Midnight.

Jennie stretched and yawned. "Well, well, if it isn't Cinderella. Out with Prince Charming again?"

Heather closed the window and pulled down the blinds. "Eric told me about the little talk you had with him. That was sneaky, Jennie."

"Maybe it runs in the family. I just put two and two together. What I don't understand is why the big secret? Why don't you just tell your folks how you feel?"

"I've tried. Dad is totally against my being a model. If they knew about Eric and me, they'd . . . I don't know what they'd do. Please don't tell Mom. She'll tell Dad and . . ."

"So when do you plan on letting them know?"

"Soon. Eric has been doing photo shoots. He's got this fantastic layout. Oh, Jennie, he's a wonderful photographer. Wait until you see them. Once the photos start selling and I get some work, we'll have enough money to get married."

"Married?" Jennie snuggled back under the covers wishing she hadn't heard Heather's response. "Just for the record, I think you're making a big mistake." She sighed. "I won't say anything right now, but I'm not making any promises."

"You sound like my grandfather."

"He knows about Eric?"

"He knows I want to be a model and that I want to leave Dancing Waters." She sat on the bed and removed her boots. "He probably knows about Eric too."

"Why doesn't he tell your folks?"

"He says I am nearing womanhood and must make my own way." Heather closed her eyes, then brushed away the tears that had formed there. "Papa says I am at a fork in the road and I must be careful in the choosing."

"So you haven't made up your mind?"

She shook her head. "I love Eric. And I love modeling. But today—when I took those people into the wilderness, I felt . . . different. Riding through the woods felt so right."

Heather changed into a plaid flannel nightshirt that reached almost to her knees. After a trip to the bathroom, she crawled into bed and turned off the light. "Good night."

" 'Night."

"Jennie?"

"Hmm?"

"Thanks for understanding."

"Sure," Jennie murmured. She didn't like sharing secrets

like that, but she no longer felt as responsible. Heather's grandfather knew. She hadn't met Joseph White Cloud yet, but she already liked him.

After lunch in the lodge the following day, Maggie gave Jennie the afternoon off. "You've earned it. Besides, Amber thinks it's time you rode into the hills to visit Papa."

"He wants to meet you." Amber turned to her mom. "May I be excused, please? I need to pick up snacks and have Dusty get the horses ready."

"Yes, you may go." She watched Amber run out the door, and shook her head. "That girl. So much energy."

The gesture reminded Jennie of something her mother would do. "Oh no. I haven't called Mom back yet. I can't believe it."

"It's my fault. I should have reminded you last night before you went to bed." Maggie set her napkin on the table. "Why don't you call her now? You can use the phone in my office."

Jennie gulped down the rest of her milk and excused herself. Minutes later she was listening to the ring and waiting for Mom to pick up the phone.

"Hello." The break in the familiar voice told Jennie her mother was crying.

"Mom, what's wrong?"

"Oh, honey. It's so awful. I'm afraid we're going to lose Hannah!"

6

"What do you mean, lose Hannah?" An image of the little girl flooded Jennie's mind. Flaxen curls and heart-melting chocolate brown eyes. "Is she sick?"

"She's fine—physically. She cried when they took her."

"Took her?" Jennie shouted into the phone. "What do you mean? Who took her? Mom, what's going on?"

Mom sniffed and blew her nose. "Her case worker came this morning. Hannah's dad wants her back."

"No! They can't do that—can they?" The idea of Hannah going back to that terrible man repulsed Jennie. He didn't deserve to have his little girl back. He'd beaten his wife and . . . Jennie shoved the horrible images away. "You can't let him take her."

"We're doing what we can. Michael and I are seeing an attorney this afternoon."

Michael Rhodes was Mom's fiancé. The thought of him being involved brought some peace of mind. If anyone could stop them, he could. Being a youth director, he'd dealt with social workers before. He'd know what to do to get Hannah back.

"I don't think Children's Services will let Chuck take her," Mom went on, "but they're talking about sending her to Arizona to live with his parents."

"Maybe I should come home." Jennie hated being so far

away. Mom probably needed a hug. Nick would be devastated.

"There's nothing you could do here. Besides, Maggie needs help and—" Mom took a deep breath as if she was about to say something Jennie didn't want to hear. "Honey, we have to remember that Hannah doesn't belong to us. We basically have no claim to her."

"Sounds like you're giving up."

"I'm just facing reality. I want to keep her as much as you do—so does Michael."

"How does Gram feel about this? Is she going with you?"

"No." Mom hesitated. "Gram is out of town. I don't think she'll be back until next week."

"Oh, I was hoping she'd come here. It's a great resort. She could write an article about it."

"Jennie, are you homesick?"

"Of course not. I just thought Gram would enjoy it." No way was Jennie going to tell Mom what she really wanted Gram there for.

"I'll mention it if she calls."

They talked a few more minutes and hung up. Jennie grabbed some tissues out of the box on her aunt's desk and blew her nose.

"Jennie, what's wrong?" Maggie came in and closed the door.

Jennie explained as best she could. "It isn't fair. She's just a little girl."

Maggie put her arms around Jennie and held her. "I know. Life often isn't fair. Sometimes it's downright cruel."

Jennie felt suddenly ashamed. They hadn't even lost Hannah yet, but Maggie and Jeff had been through so much.

Amber pulled open the door. "I got the horses ready. . . . Hey, what's going on? Did you hurt yourself?"

"No." Jennie didn't feel like going through the story again. "Would you tell her?"

Maggie did and added, "Jennie's sad about Hannah and might not feel like going for a ride."

"But everything's ready. Besides, when I'm sad, riding makes me feel better."

Jennie hauled in a ton of air and blew it out again. "I'll go. It'll beat sitting around here feeling sorry for myself."

Within a few minutes, riding had put Jennie in a better mood. Her horse would have made a good psychiatrist. While she talked, Gabby listened and even made all the appropriate sounds. A nod here, a head shake there, and exactly the right amount of snorting and whinnying.

The news about Hannah still upset her, but after talking it over with Amber and Gabby, Jennie realized that Mom was right. Being at home wouldn't change matters. She just had to trust that God would work everything out right.

With Amber acting as trail guide, they headed toward the northwest corner of the White Cloud property where Joseph lived. They'd ridden about twenty minutes through the woods when they reached a fenced clearing. Several llamas grazing near the gate straightened and fixed curious gazes on them.

Amber twisted around in her saddle and waited for Jennie to catch up. "We have about a hundred head of llamas out here."

"Why do you separate them?" Jennie asked. "I noticed several by the stables."

"We keep several near the ranch for packing."

"Packing? You eat them too?"

Amber giggled. "I meant putting packs on them for wilderness treks. They're sure-footed and better than horses on some of the steeper trails."

"No offense, Cinni." Amber reached forward to pat the horse's neck, urging her forward. The name fit her. She glistened like warm cinnamon-and-sugar coating on a sticky bun.

They rode along the fence until they came to a gate that crossed a dirt road. They dismounted, led the horses through, secured the gate, then mounted and rode on.

"I can't believe how huge this place is," Jennie said, looking over the clearing and up into the foothills. "How much land do you own?"

"Twenty-thousand acres."

Jennie let out a long whistle. "That much land must be worth millions."

"The land belongs to Papa." Amber frowned. "Some of the people around here think Papa stole the land from the Elliots. They used to live here. Now that mean Chad Elliot is telling people that Dancing Waters belongs to him. He's lying though, 'cause Papa would never steal anything."

Enemies. Marty had said the White Clouds had a lot of them. "Do you think this Elliot guy could have . . ." Jennie stopped before mentioning the explosion. *This is not the conversation to be having with a ten-year-old,* Jennie reminded herself. Even though Amber sometimes sounded like an adult, she was still very much a child. "Never mind." Then hoping to cheer her cousin, Jennie said, "You probably don't need to worry. After all, your dad's a lawyer—I'll bet he's dealt with a lot of land disputes."

Amber sighed. "I hope so."

They rode along in silence for a while as Jennie tried to bring some kind of order to the bits and pieces of the clues she'd managed to glean so far. Chad Elliot was accusing the White Clouds of stealing his land. Could he have caused the explosion? Jennie definitely needed more information, but at least now she had some specific questions.

How did Joseph White Cloud, a Nez Perce Indian chief, come to own this much land? And who wanted that land bad enough to kill for it? Her pulse quickened, hoping Amber's grandfather would have some answers.

After a few minutes, they paused to admire a hillside

ablaze with Indian Paintbrush. Amber pointed out several other plants. "These are pretty, but you should see it in the spring. The pastures are covered with Bitterroot. That's how the valley got its name."

"The Montana state flower, right? I read about it on the map."

Amber nodded. "The Indians call it 'spetlum.' They used to eat the root. Papa told me an old Indian legend about how the flower came to be. Want to hear it?"

"Sure."

Amber's expressive eyes glistened with importance as she sat straighter in the saddle and cleared her throat. "In ancient times, an old woman slipped away one night, thinking that if she were gone, the family could have her share of the little food they had. After walking a long way, the woman stopped beside a brook and loosened her long silver hair. Soon she would sing her death song. The woman thought about her family and cried with deep sorrow."

Amber gracefully raised her hand to the sky. "The Great Spirit saw her unselfish act of courage and smiled. He honored her by sending a spirit bird whose breast was red as blood. The bird promised that she and her tribe would be saved. Food would come in the form of a flower with leaves the color of her silver hair and blossoms as red as the bird's breast. The roots would be bitter as the tears she had cried and filled with the strength she carried in her heart. Each spring the flowers came to give food to her hungry people. And they continue to bloom to this day."

"What a neat story, and you told it beautifully."

"Papa says I will become the family historian. He's teaching me to be a storyteller like him so I can pass our heritage on to our children and grandchildren."

"That's a great idea. . . ."

"Shh." Amber pulled Cinnamon up and signaled Jennie to be quiet, then pointed to a small clearing. Sun streaked through the branches of the giant fir trees, making it look like a holy place. A deer nibbled at a low shrub. She raised her head and looked straight at them. Jennie expected her to bolt. Instead she came toward Cinnamon and nuzzled Amber's saddlebags.

Amber slowly reached into the bag. The deer stretched out her neck and accepted the cookie Amber offered.

"She's beautiful." Jennie pulled a cookie out of her bag, too.

"Her name's Tasha. Papa found her when she was a fawn. A hunter killed her mother."

"Sounds like a Bambi story." Jennie leaned farther forward and extended her hand. "Here, Tasha." The doe ambled over and snatched the cookie Jennie offered.

Amber nodded. "Hunters aren't allowed here, but sometimes they come anyway. I worry about her."

"And well you should, Tiponi," a deep mellow voice said. "Tasha is young and has not yet learned to fear humans. If she is to live long enough to see her children grow, she must know this fear."

Startled by the voice, Jennie yanked on Gabby's reins. The horse sidestepped and reared, throwing her off balance. She grabbed for the saddlehorn with her casted right hand and missed. She yelped as she tumbled from the saddle and landed on her rear.

Tasha darted into the underbrush. Gabby turned and nuzzled Jennie as if to apologize.

A figure appeared in the haloed light and came toward her. "I frightened you. I'm sorry. Are you hurt?"

Still dazed, Jennie took the hand he offered and scrambled to her feet. Her fear melted the moment his steady gaze caught hers. "I—I don't think so." She brushed off the dirt and debris from the forest floor. Her leg and tailbone still hurt, but the pain was beginning to subside.

"It's my fault, Papa." Amber swung her legs to the side

and slid off Cinnamon's back. "I should have warned her about the way you sneak up on people."

He chuckled, then bent to embrace her. Amber kissed his brown furrowed cheek and hugged him. He wore a feather, Jennie noticed, a brown one with a white tip, tucked into the long gray braid that hung down his back. She'd expected him to be dressed like an Indian chief, in a feathered headdress and buckskin, but he wasn't. In his faded blue jeans and aqua chambray work shirt he looked like a typical rancher. Joseph gathered Gabby's and Cinnamon's reins in one hand and began walking. "Come, my children. I have been expecting you. I have made your favorite, Tiponi. Frybread. We will eat and share stories. I am eager to hear about Jennie and her family."

"And I want to hear about yours." Jennie took Amber's hand and fell into step in front of Joseph and the horses. "Why does he call you that strange name?" Jennie asked Amber.

"Tiponi? That's my Indian name." Her eyes widened and her lips parted in a wide smile. "It means 'child of importance.'"

"Tiponi. It's a beautiful name, and you know what? It fits."

"I know." Amber couldn't have beamed more if she'd have been a light bulb. "Maybe Papa will give you a name."

"Actually, Gram gave me one. Not a name exactly, but she says I'm like an eagle—steady and strong."

"It suits you," Joseph said. "Your grandmother sounds like a wise woman."

"She is."

As they walked, Jennie answered more questions about her family. Since he already knew about the Calhoun side— her mom and Uncle Kevin—she told him about the Mc-Gradys. Gram first, of course, and how she'd been married to Ian McGrady, a government agent who'd been killed nearly eleven years ago. Joseph seemed disappointed when Jennie told him Gram had recently married again.

When Joseph asked, she told him about her father, from whom she'd inherited her height, dark hair, and cobalt blue eyes.

"We're almost there," Amber announced, then ran ahead of them. Jennie dropped back and walked beside Joseph.

"Maggie tells me you are quite a detective," Joseph said. "This, I have seen for myself."

It took Jennie a moment to realize what he was referring to. "Oh, you mean the other night. You had me going there. I thought God had sent an angel."

His eyes twinkled. "Not an angel, but certainly an assistant. I was coming home from visiting a friend."

So the voice she'd heard in the woods had belonged to him. "Did you have to be so sneaky? Why didn't you just come out and tell me how to get back?"

Joseph had the smile of a man with many secrets. "If a child is always carried, he will never learn to walk."

"You mean if you had shown me the way, I wouldn't have learned to make it on my own. I wouldn't have learned how to listen to the earth."

"Or to your spirit." Their path ended at a rustic log cabin that looked as old as he did.

"Papa, Papa." Amber ran back to them, tears running down her cheeks.

"Hush, Tiponi." He knelt and pressed her head against his chest. "What has upset you?"

"They killed her," she sobbed and glanced toward the house. "They killed Tasha."

7

Jennie couldn't look. She closed her eyes, but still caught a glimpse of the white tail and rounded belly that lay on the ground near the far side of the cabin.

"How—how could . . ." Jennie stammered. "I—I didn't hear a shot."

"They must have used a silencer. Stay here with Tiponi while I check around." Joseph positioned Jennie and Amber beside a dark green Ford Ranger and ran into the house.

Glancing inside the vehicle, Jennie noticed a cellular phone. She could call for help if— Her thoughts dissipated as Joseph emerged from the house.

"Go inside and wait for me," he ordered. "Lock the door."

She and Amber sat at the kitchen table and waited. Only then did Jennie relax enough to notice her surroundings. A southwestern-style rug stretched from the sofa to a couple of matching leather chairs. Next to the fire stood an old wooden rocker with a worn cloth cushion. Tired of sitting, Jennie decided to explore.

The log cabin looked bigger from the inside. The main room served as a sitting room, kitchen, and eating area. A circular fire pit occupied the center of the room. Smoke from the fire escaped through a metal vent that looked like an upside-down funnel—narrow at the top where it met the ceiling. At one end of the room were three open doors leading to two bedrooms and a bath.

The furnishings were old, and Jennie took her time examining them. In one bedroom, a framed picture of Christ knocking at a door hung beside an embroidery of the Twenty-third Psalm. An antique Bible sat on a stand below the picture.

Thirty minutes passed before they saw Joseph again. His hands were covered with dirt and blood. "It was not Tasha," he said going to the kitchen sink. "This one was older. One of the poachers must have wounded it, then lost the trail."

Amber sighed. "I'm glad it wasn't her. Are you going to call the sheriff?"

"You must not concern yourself with these matters."

Jennie might have believed Joseph's explanation about the poacher except for two things. He hadn't looked into her eyes, and he had a piece of pale green paper in his shirt pocket that hadn't been there earlier. The paper had a frayed edge just like the one left on Heather's Jeep. When he turned around after washing his hands, the paper was gone.

Joseph excused himself to shower and change clothes, then went into his bedroom.

Jennie wondered what he'd done with the note. Maybe he'd show it to her later. Or maybe he'd already thrown it away.

Jennie looked over at the sink where Joseph had been standing, then pushed her chair back and casually sauntered into the kitchen. She opened the cupboard and checked the trash. Bingo. Her hunch had been right. She pulled out the crinkled bloodstained note and read it.

This could be you. Jennie folded the note and jammed it into the pocket of her jeans. Later she'd compare the handwriting. She wondered how many threatening notes the White Clouds had gotten and how many they'd handed over to the sheriff.

She headed to the leather sofa and sank into it. Amber, who'd been curled up in the armchair, got up, took a piece of firewood from a box beside the pit, and placed it in the ashes. "I hate it when deer get killed. I wish people couldn't hunt anymore. And I wish I was the sheriff. I'd round up all the hunters and put them in jail."

Jennie glanced at the mounted moose head with antlers nearly as wide as the room. "Your grandfather hunts. Would you put him in jail too?"

"That's different. Papa says the Creator gives us plants and animals for food and clothing. Some of the hunters are like Papa, but most of the poachers do it for fun. They use high-powered rifles and automatic weapons. . . ."

Joseph came out of his bedroom. "Tiponi," he scolded, "how do you know these things? Did your father tell you this?"

Amber shrugged. "I hear things, Papa. And I know."

Joseph pinched his lips together. His obsidian eyes clouded with concern, but he said no more about it. Instead he turned and walked into the kitchen area and pulled a piece of white cloth from a large lump of dough.

Joseph dropped pieces of the dough out on a floured cutting board and patted them until they were flat and round. One by one he formed them, slid them into a black iron skillet with hot oil to fry, then set them aside to drain.

Within a few minutes they were feasting on warm frybread, spread with butter and dripping with brilliant red strawberry jam.

Jennie, too warm to stay near the fire, chose a seat next to the large window in the living room. She gazed at the trees and a meadow dotted with colorful wild flowers. Like Jeff and Maggie's home, Joseph's had a great view. Here, though, you didn't just look at the mountains, you were in them.

"This is a wonderful place. It looks old."

"My father built it in 1901 when he married my mother.

Except for the wood floor and the fire pit I put in for Chenoa in 1948, it is the same."

"Chenoa? Your wife?" Jennie asked. She loved the sound of the Indian names.

Joseph nodded. His black eyes drifted closed in an almost reverent gesture.

"Papa and Daddy were both born in that bedroom back there." Amber pointed to an open door on the right. A worn, multicolor handmade quilt covered the bed.

"The quilt—did Chenoa make it?"

Joseph opened his eyes and looked toward the room. "A wedding gift from Nadi—my mother."

Jennie wanted to explore every inch of the cabin—to pick up each item and learn its history. It was like being in a museum.

"Come," Joseph said. "You have many questions. Too many for an old man to answer. But I will begin with the story of my people."

Joseph led them away from the cabin to a cleared grassy knoll overlooking the valley. A cemetery, Jennie realized as they drew closer. They stopped near five marble tombstones. Joseph sat on a rough-hewn log bench, looked briefly at each marker, then let his gaze move over the valley and down to the river.

Jennie read the writing on each stone. *Gray Wolf 1846–77*; *Dancing Waters 1849–1877*; *White Cloud 1872–1972*; *Nadi 1901–1971*; *Chenoa 1927–1988*. She pointed to Dancing Waters' tomb. "Who was this?"

"The ranch was named for her." Amber tucked several stray tendrils behind her ear, crossed her legs at the ankle, and dropped down next to her grandfather. "She was Gray Wolf's sister."

"You know of the Nez Perce, Jennie?" Joseph asked.

"Yes—some. I studied about Chief Joseph in school."

"Ah." He nodded. "I am named for Chief Joseph and for his father, Old Joseph."

"Are you related to them?"

"Not by blood, but they are my brothers. My great-grandfather was Chief Gray Wolf. He and Chief Joseph were friends and sought to maintain peaceful relations with the settlers. Unfortunately that was not to be. The settlers and miners wanted more and more of our land, especially after gold was discovered on the reservation in 1860."

Jennie sighed. "I remember reading about that. The government drew up a new treaty reducing the reservation to a tenth its original size." Jennie shook her head. "It all seems so unfair."

"At the time, we were considered savages. As Chief Joseph said, 'we were few, they were many. We were like deer. They were like grizzly bears. . . . We were content to let things remain as the Great Spirit Chief made them. They were not; and would change the rivers and mountains if they did not suit them.' "

"Tell her about the war, Papa." Amber leaned toward him.

"Patience, Tiponi." He chuckled and pulled her closer. "Perhaps Jennie already knows about the war."

"She doesn't know about our part," Amber protested.

"I do know about the Nez Perce War—the Battle at Big Hole in . . . um . . . 18—something."

"Yes. 1877. The battle was fought not far from here." Joseph pointed to a distant mountain range to the east.

"Papa's great-grandfather, Gray Wolf, was killed and so was Dancing Waters. Tell her, Papa."

"Since you are so eager, Tiponi, perhaps you should tell your cousin the story of our ancestors."

"Okay. But you tell me if I make a mistake."

"You won't," Jennie assured her as she shifted to find a more comfortable position. To Joseph she said, "You should have heard her tell me about the Bitterroot legend. You'd have been proud."

"Of Tiponi, I am always proud."

"Well," Amber straightened with the importance her name implied and began, "Gray Wolf was camped here in the valley with his sister, Dancing Waters, and his five-year-old son, White Cloud. White Cloud's mama died right after he was born. Gray Wolf and Dancing Waters became friends with Frank Elliot, the man who used to own this land.

"Mr. Elliot thought Dancing Waters was the most beautiful girl in the world and wanted to marry her." Amber sighed and shrugged her shoulders. "Dancing Waters loved him too, but she was already promised to . . . um . . . What was his name, Papa?"

"Red Fox."

"Oh, yeah. Anyway, several of the young warriors got mad because the settlers and miners kept taking their land. They killed some settlers and got all the Indians in trouble. The Nez Perce tried to avoid battle, but the soldiers kept coming after them.

"Lots of people died in the war at Big Hole." Amber glanced at Joseph. "How many, Papa?"

"Twenty-nine soldiers dead, forty wounded." Joseph paused. His sad gaze settled on the first two graves. "The Nez Perce won the battle, but lost as well. Eighty-two of our people died. Most of them were women, children, and old people."

"Dancing Waters died in the battle," Amber went on, "and Gray Wolf was wounded. Frank Elliot heard about the fighting and came the next day. He took Gray Wolf and little White Cloud, but Gray Wolf died the next day. Frank promised Gray Wolf that he would take care of White Cloud forever."

Jennie frowned, remembering what Amber had told her

earlier. "If Frank owned all of this land, how did you come to own it?"

"Does it surprise you?" Joseph asked.

"No—Well, I guess it does," Jennie admitted.

"Frank Elliot was a good man. He reared my father against the advice of many in the valley who thought Indians belonged on the reservation. Two years after the war, Frank married a young woman whose father had made a fortune in the mining industry.

"At first she accepted White Cloud and cared for him, but eventually she bore children of her own, and became jealous of the attention her husband paid to White Cloud. In an attempt to pacify his wife, and still keep his promise, Frank gave White Cloud five hundred acres.

"Frank's children, William and Tess, grew up spoiled and bitter." Joseph went on. "When Frank died, William took to alcohol and gambling. Heavy losses caused him to sell parcels of the land to my father and later to me. He asked us to keep the land deals a secret so that he could buy it back, but that day never came."

"And the family never knew?"

"Perhaps they never cared. Sale of the land brought in money. The money is gone now. William's grandson, Chad, has come back to claim the land he believes is his."

The old man sighed, looking weary and somehow older and more frail than when they'd first met. He stood and straightened slowly. "We have no more time for questions. I promised Maggie I'd send you home by four-thirty."

Reluctantly, Jennie and Amber headed for home. Late afternoon shadows stretched across the trail and dropped the temperature a good twenty degrees. They'd ridden about a mile and had just entered the llama pastures when a strange uneasiness settled in the pit of Jennie's stomach. The hair on the back of her neck bristled in warning.

"Amber, hold on a minute." She pulled back on the reins

and reached out to touch her cousin's arm, then scanned the area.

"What is it, Jennie?"

"I don't know. Something doesn't feel right. I know it sounds dumb, but I feel like we're being watched."

Amber grinned. "It's probably Papa. He sometimes follows me to make sure I get home okay."

Jennie relaxed some. "Maybe. Still, we should be careful." She sat high on Gabby's back and looked over the pasture again.

Just as Amber started forward Jennie saw him—a dark figure kneeling beside a large outcropping of rocks. His camouflage fatigues nearly hid him from view. He raised his rifle and looked through the scope.

"He's going to kill one of the llamas!" Amber cried. Before Jennie could stop her, Amber spurred Cinnamon forward. "Hey!" she yelled. "This is private property. What do you think you're doing?"

The man looked toward them. A black ski mask covered his face. He stood and swung the rifle around, then set his sights on Amber.

8

"No!" Jennie yelled as she urged Gabby forward. "Amber, wait!"

Amber didn't stop until she reached the rocks where they'd seen the gunman. "He's gone."

Jennie glanced around. "He hasn't had time to go far. We'd better get out of here."

"He was going to shoot the llamas. It's a good thing we came."

Jennie heard the roar of an engine. She dug her heels into Gabby's sides and raced toward the sound. By the time she reached the road leading out of the pasture, the truck, resembling an old army reject, rammed the gate and disappeared down the winding dirt road. She'd tried to read the license plate, but a billowing dust cloud obliterated her view.

"Let's follow him," Amber said as she caught up with Jennie. "See where he goes."

They rode as far as the gate when Jennie stopped her. "It's no use. We'll never catch him."

Amber jumped off Cinnamon and walked over to the broken gate. "We'd better fix this so the llamas don't get out."

The truck had splintered the two center posts and snapped the barbed wire. Amber picked up the broken gate and twisted the ends of the wires together. Jennie then helped her stretch the wires taut and hook a wire loop over a secure post.

"I wish we could have caught him," Amber said.

"Jennie stooped to pick up some pieces of glass and wood splinters.

"What are you doing?"

"Gathering evidence." She found a tissue in her jacket pocket and carefully wrapped the fragments, then inserted them in the pocket of her jean jacket. Judging from the amount of glass strewn about, he must have broken a headlight.

"We're lucky he didn't kill us." Jennie brushed the dirt from her hands. "Don't you know any better than to chase after guys with guns?"

Amber pursed her lips in a pout. "I didn't think about him hurting us. I was worried about the llamas."

Jennie hooked her left arm around Amber's neck and hugged her. "I know. You're a lot like me. Sometimes I act first and think later. Anyway, we'd better get going. We need to call the sheriff. I got a pretty good look at the truck. The sheriff should be able to find it. How many people around here have trucks like that?"

Amber sniffed. "Lots. The sheriff won't find him. He probably won't even try."

"I don't understand," Jennie said as they mounted their horses.

"Um . . . There's like this Montana Militia. I don't know much about them except they don't like us. They look like army guys. Papa and Daddy have been trying to keep them off our property. They think they have a right to be here 'cause the Elliots' caretaker let them use the ranch for their war games."

"War games?" Jennie felt sick. She'd been hearing a lot about militia groups since the bombing in Oklahoma. *Bombing.* Uncle Jeff had been injured in an explosion, and she'd seen several men in army fatigues since she'd arrived in Montana.

Including Marty's father. Only that morning, Maggie had suspected Mr. Danielson of cutting the fence bordering his property. Could he have been the man they'd just seen?

"Amber, do you know the Danielsons very well?"

"A little. Before the explosion, Mr. Danielson was always coming over to talk to Dad—well, argue mostly. Marty was Heather's boyfriend when we first came here. I don't like him."

"Who, Marty?"

"No, his dad."

They reached the stable at five-fifteen and told Dusty what had happened. Dusty called the sheriff and hustled the girls over to the lodge office.

A few minutes later, they told the story to Maggie, who scolded, fed, and hugged them, then asked Heidi to take Amber to the house while she and Jennie waited. Forty-five minutes later, the sheriff pulled up in front of the lodge office where Maggie had suggested they meet.

The sheriff stuffed his ample body into an armchair, laced his fingers together, and rested them on his belly. "Well, now, little lady. Suppose you tell me about this gunman of yours and why you felt it was so all-fired important for me to drive all the way out here." His tone implied Jennie had dreamed the whole thing up. She could see why Heather questioned his competence.

Jennie repeated the story, emphasizing the mask and the gun. "It looked like an assault weapon."

"Is that everything?"

"No, it isn't." She struggled to keep the irritation out of her voice. "He got away in a camouflaged truck." Jennie described the vehicle.

"Well, now we're getting somewhere." He gave Maggie a snide grin, then shifted his gaze back to Jennie. "Have you any idea how many folks in this county drive camouflaged trucks?"

"No, but this one would have a broken headlight and probably wood splinters caught in the bumper from the fence. I picked up a couple of pieces when I was out there." She retrieved the wood and glass from her pocket and handed them to him. "It shouldn't be hard to check out some of the trucks around here. You could start with the Danielsons."

"Now, don't be telling me how to do my job, little lady." Sheriff Mason set down his coffee cup and stood. He hooked a finger on either side of his tan pants and hitched them up. The handle of his gun made a dent in his bulging stomach. "I've heard tell how you assisted the police in Oregon with a couple of cases, but you'd better not be gettin' any ideas about doin' that here."

Before Jennie could reply, he turned to Maggie. "I'm right sorry about all the trouble you folks been havin' out here. I know seeing a fella like that can be alarmin', but my hunch is, the girls just surprised a hunter."

Maggie's angry gaze flitted to Jennie then back to the sheriff. "That gunman was no hunter, Sam Mason, and you know it. He was on our land. He aimed a gun at our llamas and at our children. I expect you to investigate this. I want that lunatic caught."

"Now, Maggie." Sheriff Mason straightened and backed away. "Don't be getting your dander up. All I'm saying is, this guy's probably one of the militia boys that didn't get the message about Dancing Waters bein' off limits now that the Elliots are gone. I'll ask around, but don't expect an arrest." The sheriff huffed. "Like findin' a blasted needle in a haystack. I don't have the manpower for wild goose chases like this."

"He's not going to do anything, is he?" Jennie asked after the sheriff left.

"Of course he will. Sheriff Mason is up for election soon.

69

He can't afford to slack off too much."

"I hope you're right."

Maggie motioned for Jennie to join her on the porch. "Come on. Walk with me up to the house. I want to check on Amber."

As they trudged up the hill, they talked about family matters and how Maggie hadn't felt like part of the family for the first dozen or so years of her marriage to Jeff. Jennie asked why.

"You mean you never heard the story?"

"Not your version. All I heard was that you were a rebellious hippie teenager and you ran off with an Indian. Mom never talked about you much."

"My fault. I guess I didn't feel welcome. Basically, the story is true. Jeff and I fell in love and wanted to get married. My parents wanted me to finish college and marry some wealthy businessman. I wanted Jeff. So we eloped. We had such high ideals—thought we could save the world. The twins were born a year later, and caring for them pretty much ended our political activist days. Not that I'm complaining; I love being a mother.

"For the longest time I was too hurt and full of pride to come home. Then at your father's funeral . . ." Tears misted her eyes and Maggie reached up to brush them away. "Listen to me going on like that. The past isn't important. What counts now is that all is forgiven. The prodigal daughter has returned to the fold."

"I'm glad you made up with Grandma and Grandpa Calhoun—and Mom and Uncle Kevin. Mom really missed you."

"I'm glad too." She rested an arm on Jennie's shoulder. "And I can't wait until that sister of mine gets here. We have so much catching up to do."

The phone rang as they walked into the kitchen.

"Hello," Maggie grabbed it on the first ring. She frowned.

"Yes, she's here. Just a second." Maggie handed the phone to Jennie. "It's Marty."

"How's it going?" Marty asked after they exchanged greetings. "Heard you spooked some hunter this afternoon and almost got yourself shot at."

"Where'd you hear about that?" Jennie asked. Suspicions so crowded her brain she could hardly hear his answer.

"Sheriff Mason. He dropped by to ask if we'd seen anything."

"Have you?" Jennie asked, surprised the sheriff had been there.

"Nope."

Jennie had a dozen questions to shoot at Marty Danielson. *Where were you this afternoon? Where was your father? Hit any fences with your truck lately?* She couldn't very well ask those over the phone for fear he'd hang up, so she didn't say anything.

Marty finally broke the awkward silence. "I . . . um . . . I guess you're wondering why I called."

"Yeah, now that you mention it."

"I just got to thinking about you. I'm free this evening and was wondering if maybe we could get together. I can show you around our ranch, then we can head into town and see a movie or get a hamburger or something."

"Sure. That would be terrific. I'd love to see your place." *And,* she thought, *look over your vehicles.*

"Great. I'll pick you up at seven."

After she hung up, Jennie began to wonder about the wisdom of her decision. What if the gunman had been Marty or his dad? If the sheriff had told them about the cases she'd helped solve recently, they might want her out of the way. Okay, maybe she shouldn't have accepted the invitation, but going to the Danielsons' would give her an opportunity to snoop around. For tonight, Jennie would play the part of a city girl enjoying a night out on the town with a handsome cowboy. Considering everything, she could have thought of worse ways to spend an evening.

Besides, she doubted Marty was involved. When they'd talked on the plane, he'd seemed surprised and sad when she told him about the explosion. *You're taking a big risk here, McGrady. You'd better hope your intuition is riding on the right trail.*

9

"I take it you're going out."

Jennie spun around. She'd forgotten about Maggie. "Um . . . Aunt Maggie, it's not what you think. I met Marty on the plane." She winced. "I'm sorry, I should have asked you first. If you don't want me to go, I can call him back."

"No. It's okay." Maggie frowned. "Just be careful, okay?" She stopped and took a deep breath, then smiled. "With all that's happening around here I've become rather paranoid. You go on ahead and have a good time."

"Um, Aunt Maggie. I know Heather used to date Marty and . . . well, you don't think she'd mind, do you?"

"Oh, I doubt it, Jennie. They haven't gone out in a long while."

"Well, I guess I'd better shower. I look like I've been rolling in dirt and smell like horse sweat."

"I'll leave you to it, then." Maggie started to leave, then turned back around. "Oh, Jennie. I meant to tell you. I'll be bringing Jeff home tonight. The doctor said I'd better come get him before all the nurses quit. He'll be happier here anyway where he can monitor things."

"Tonight? Are you sure you don't want me to stay?"

Maggie shook her head. "No need. I'll be taking Amber with me and it'll be late when we get back. I just wanted to warn you."

"Warn me?" Jennie frowned.

"He may not be in the best frame of mind. You see, he didn't want me to ask you and Susan to come. He doesn't like asking for help. If he seems . . . well, angry, it isn't that he's upset with you. He's blaming himself for everything that's happened."

Jennie smiled. "Don't worry about me, Aunt Maggie." The desire to find the person or persons responsible for the explosion burned in her heart with renewed intensity.

Maggie hugged her again, then went into the kitchen while Jennie hurried upstairs to shower.

Not knowing what to wear on a date with a cowboy, Jennie decided to go for the casual look, with a white long-sleeved shirt and jeans. She transferred the threatening notes to her clean jeans and slipped on her jean jacket. *You should have given the notes to the sheriff,* she reminded herself. Then again, maybe that wasn't the best idea. Jennie didn't trust him any more than Heather did.

She lifted strands of her limp, wet hair, wondering what to do with it. Maybe Maggie would braid it. Grabbing her brush and an elastic band along with one of Heather's feather barrettes, Jennie headed downstairs in search for her aunt, or someone who had the use of two hands.

True to his word, Marty picked Jennie up at seven in a red Dodge truck. Wearing a cowboy hat, cream-colored shirt, denim jacket, Wrangler jeans, and boots, he looked as ruggedly handsome as he had on the plane. His broad smile chased away any lingering doubts about his involvement—almost.

A tour of Double D ranch provided no clues. Jennie saw four vehicles but none of them resembled the truck she'd seen in the llama pasture. Maybe she'd been too hasty in suspecting Marty's dad.

On the other hand, Marty had hurried her past one of the out-buildings. He'd called it a machine shed. "Just full of old machinery parts and tools," he'd told her.

She'd thought about telling him she loved tools, then decided against it. No sense being too obvious. Maybe later she'd take Gabby out, sneak over and check out the shop herself.

The tour ended with the Danielsons' modest log home. "Where are your folks?" Jennie asked after she'd been through the house.

Marty shrugged and led her outside. "Probably in town. Mom wanted to go out for dinner."

Marty leaned against one of the support beams on the porch. "Seen enough?"

"I guess. I like your place—it's homey. Have you lived here long?"

"All my life. You sure ask a lot of questions, Jennie McGrady. What gives?"

Jennie flashed him what she hoped was an innocent smile. "Just curious. I've always asked a lot of questions. Mom says I drove her and Dad nuts when I was little. Anyway, I grew up in the city and all this country stuff fascinates me. I want to learn as much as I can."

Marty must have taken her remark as a compliment. His grin widened as he pushed away from the post and hung an arm around her neck. "Then ask away. Let's head into town—see what kind of trouble we can get into."

"Trouble?"

He chuckled. "Just kidding. Thought maybe we'd do a little line dancing—listen to the band down at Willie's."

Jennie stopped. "Um . . . Willie's? That's not some kind of tavern is it? I mean . . . I'm only sixteen. And I'm not much into dancing. I have absolutely no coordination. I'm sure it's because I'm so tall. Takes too long for messages to travel from my brain to my feet."

He grabbed her hand and pulled her toward the truck. "Not to worry. They don't serve anything stronger than Sarsaparilla. People who own it named it after Willie Nelson. Guess he was there once."

————

For the next two hours, Marty showed Jennie around town and introduced her to at least a dozen friends.

Several of the guys at Willie's wore fatigues, similar to those Marty's dad had worn at the restaurant. Probably members of the militia group Amber had told her about, but Jennie wanted to hear Marty's explanation. "What's the deal with so many of the guys around here wearing military fatigues? Is there an army base around here?"

Marty glanced up at the men in question, his blue eyes registering disapproval. "They're in an army all right, but not Uncle Sam's." He shifted his gaze back to Jennie. "No more questions, okay? We came here to relax and have some fun." Without giving her a chance to answer, he grabbed her hand and pulled her across the room. "Come on, let's pick out a song on the jukebox. Who's your favorite country singer?"

"I don't really have a favorite," Jennie said, deciding to put her questions on hold. For the next hour or so, they ate, talked, laughed, listened to country music, and drank sodas. At ten, Jennie could barely keep her eyes open, and her entire body was protesting from the unaccustomed paces she'd put it through. "I'm sorry, Marty, but I'd better get back. I'm not used to getting up so early or working so hard."

He looked disappointed, but didn't argue. On the drive back to Dancing Waters and the Double D, Marty surprised her by asking about the gunman. "You must have been pretty scared."

"You've got that right. Any idea who it might have been?"

"I told you earlier that I didn't."

"The sheriff said he was probably a hunter." Jennie shifted in her seat so she could watch his reactions. "Why would he think that?"

Marty shrugged. "It's a logical assumption. Why else would he be out there?"

"Marty, the guy had an automatic weapon. He was aiming at the llamas, wearing army fatigues and a black ski mask. That doesn't sound like any hunter I've ever seen. Amber said something about a militia group and war games."

"I know where you're going with this, but I can tell you right now that none of the militia guys around here would have caused the explosion out at Dancing Waters. For one thing, the foreman was a good friend of Dad's. They served in Nam together." Marty's hand tightened on the steering wheel. "The militia guys are mighty upset about not being able to use the property for their weekend maneuvers, but they wouldn't resort to killing—especially one of their own guys."

"How do you know one of them wouldn't? I mean, the gunman I saw today was definitely . . ."

Marty's dark look stopped her. "What? Can you positively identify him as being one of the militia guys? Anyone could buy an outfit like that. You don't know he wasn't a hunter. You probably don't even know if it was a guy."

Jennie leaned her head back against the seat. "You're right about that. For all I know it could have been you." Jennie clamped her lips together wishing she could take back the accusation. She didn't really suspect that Marty had anything to do with the explosion, only that he might know who did.

Marty sighed and stared straight ahead.

"I'm sorry. I didn't mean that."

"I think you did. You suspect my dad even more, don't you?"

Jennie shrugged. She thought about saying no, but decided to level with him. Honesty on her part might make him more apt to talk to her. "I know your dad and Uncle Jeff haven't been on good terms."

Marty laughed. "That's putting it mildly. They hate each other's guts."

"Why?"

"It's a long story."

"So, condense it for me."

"Most of it's political. Dad and his troops are ultra-conservative and anti-government. They don't like the way the country's being run and are out to change it. White Cloud is more liberal in his views. They're at each other's throats, but not literally. Dad may not love his neighbor, but he sure wouldn't kill him."

"I'm still not convinced." Jennie told him about the death threats Heather and Joseph had gotten and explained where they'd come from. "You and your dad were at the restaurant."

Marty glanced at the notes when Jennie dug them out of her pocket and held them up. "I didn't know about those. But my dad couldn't have put the note on Heather's Jeep. I was with him, remember?"

"Yes, but were you watching him the entire time?"

Silence stretched between them. Marty stared straight ahead. Was he beginning to wonder about his dad's involvement?

He slowed and flipped on the blinker as they neared the Double D. "Tell you what, Jennie. To put your mind at ease once and for all, I'm gonna take you back to the Double D to meet my dad. Maybe then you'll see why I keep defending him."

Jennie agreed. Marty had just turned off the highway when they heard a siren and saw the flashing lights behind them.

"Must be the sheriff. Wonder what he wants?" Marty eased the car onto the gravel shoulder.

"Apparently not you," Jennie said as the sheriff's car sped past.

"Something's wrong at the house." Marty whipped the truck back onto the road and raced after the patrol car.

10

Jennie jammed her feet on the floorboard and clutched the dash as Marty careened around a corner. "Slow down!" she shrieked. "Do you want to get us killed?"

"I have to get to Dad. He's got a bad heart." He slammed on the brakes and hooked a right into the Double D.

A camouflaged truck with a dented front end and a broken headlamp was parked in front of the machine shed.

Jennie stepped out of the truck and followed Marty to the porch where the sheriff was talking to Jake Danielson.

"What's going on?" Marty demanded, his jaw tight with concern.

Danielson stared at the truck. He clenched his fists and turned toward Jennie. "What's she doing here?" Jennie took a step back. She could almost feel the heat of his anger.

"This is all your doing," he yelled, jabbing a finger at Jennie. "You and them blasted Indians. Nobody sets up Jake Danielson and gets away with it. Nobody!"

Sheriff Mason ran a hand along his square jaw. "All right, Jake. Just settle down. No one's accusing you of anything. Just following up on a tip is all."

Marty glanced from the truck to his dad, his eyes glazed over with worry.

"Now let's take a look at that vehicle over there." The sheriff started walking, apparently expecting them to follow.

"Some guy called not more'n ten minutes ago. Said the camouflaged truck I was looking for was parked in your yard."

Even though the double-wide mercury light atop a pole near the house illuminated the entire yard, Sheriff Mason unsnapped a flashlight from his belt and directed the light toward the battered pickup.

"This your truck, Jake?"

Danielson swore. "You know it is. License plate'll bear that out. But I sure as heck wasn't driving it today. Haven't set foot on White Cloud's property in more'n a week."

"Well, little lady, good thing you're here. Save me the trouble of having to call you. This the truck you think you saw this afternoon?"

Jennie opened her mouth then closed it again. She glanced from Marty to Mr. Danielson, then back at the sheriff. "I didn't *think* I saw it, Sheriff. I *did* see it."

"That's not what I asked. Is this the vehicle you saw?"

"It looks like it."

He turned back to Jake. "I'm sorry about this, old buddy, but I'm going to have to get some forensics people out."

"The truck was stolen, Sam. You know that. I called your office early this morning to report it."

While the men talked, Jennie examined the rear of the truck, then walked around to the front end and knelt down to check out the dents and scratches. Pieces of wood mixed with the glass from the broken headlight were caught in the space behind the bumper and inside the broken light. Two scratches about a foot apart marred the hood. Jennie suspected they'd been caused by the barbed wire. This had to be the truck she'd seen.

She pointed out the scratches and wood chips to the sheriff. "I'm sure if you run a few tests on the wood and glass I gave you this afternoon . . ."

"Miss McGrady," the sheriff said in a patronizing tone. "I am perfectly capable of running my investigations without your interference. For your information, I collected a few samples of my own. I have little doubt that this is the truck you saw. Just wanted you to verify it." To Marty he said, "Why don't you take Jennie here back to Dancin' Waters before I haul her in for tampering with the evidence?"

Marty grabbed her elbow. "Come on," he murmured. "Let's get out of here."

"I hope you're not thinking about arresting me." Though Jake had spoken to the sheriff, he glared at Jennie.

Jennie could have said a lot of things, but she refused to stoop to Danielson's level. She clamped her lips together, shrugged Marty's hand away, then spun around and headed for his truck.

"Not at the moment," she heard Sheriff Mason answer. "Reckon I'll need to get a statement, though."

Jennie looked back at the two men as she opened the passenger-side door.

"I know."

The sheriff slapped Jake Danielson's back in a friendly sort of way. "Now what's say we go in and explain all this to Betty."

Marty didn't say much on the short drive to Dancing Waters. He seemed sad and confused. Jennie wanted to console him, but what could she say?

When they pulled up to the house, Marty caught her hand before she could open the door. "He didn't do it, Jennie. I know it looks bad, but . . ." He tipped his head back and after a sharp intake of breath said, "I don't know why I keep defending him. I mean, it's not like he isn't capable of violence. Maybe he did do it. Maybe . . ."

"Marty, I'm sorry this has happened. I hope your dad's innocent. He did say the truck had been stolen. It's possible someone's trying to pin this on him."

Marty smiled. "You really are something, Jennie. Here

my dad treats you like garbage and you're trying to make me feel better."

Jennie shrugged and looked away. "I'd better go in now. Keep me posted, okay?"

Marty nodded. "Sure. I'll call you tomorrow."

"Um . . . Marty, if you need someone to talk to about things . . . I mean . . . well, you know."

He leaned over and brushed his lips against her cheek. "Thanks."

Before going inside, Jennie turned to wave at the headlights.

The house was dark and Jennie had only the light from the moon to guide her to the porch. Where was everyone? Then she remembered that Maggie and Amber had gone into Missoula to pick up Uncle Jeff. Maybe they hadn't returned yet. Glancing over to the garage, she realized that wasn't the case. The White Clouds' station wagon sat next to the Jeep in front of the garage. Were they all sleeping?

It must have been later than she'd thought. She lifted her left arm to check her watch, but it was too dark. Jennie climbed the porch steps and went inside. She removed her shoes at the door, then tiptoed toward the stairs.

"A little late for you to be sneaking in, isn't it?" A man's harsh voice rang out in the stillness.

"Who. . . ?" Jennie whipped around. Fear exploded through her like a lightning bolt. Her heart began to quiet as she saw the silhouette of a man in a wheelchair against the silvery, moonlit window. One pajama-clad leg dangled from the chair. He seemed to be staring at something outside. Jennie took a step toward him, then stopped. Though darkness partially hid his features, his anger, almost tangible in its intensity, engulfed her like smoke from a forest fire. "I—I'm sorry, Uncle Jeff. I wanted to get here sooner, but . . ."

The cloud of fury dissipated. Jeff spun his wheelchair around and cleared his throat. "I'm the one who should apologize. I thought you were Heather."

Jennie offered him a tentative smile, closing the distance between them. If he'd been Uncle Kevin, Mom and Maggie's brother, she'd have wrapped her arms around his neck and hugged him. But here, now, Jennie held back. She'd only met him once before, at her dad's funeral.

"You went out with Marty Danielson."

The comment caught her off guard and held a strong hint of accusation. She lowered herself onto the arm of the sofa.

"I met him on the plane, and since he's your neighbor I thought he might have some insight as to what's been going on around here."

Jennie had grown accustomed to the scant light and could more easily see his features. He was a handsome man, with a square face and wide forehead which wrinkled in a frown. He wore his long dark hair pulled back in a braid like Joseph's. His eyes reminded her of Joseph's too, dark and penetrating as if they could see into her soul.

"And did you learn anything of interest?" He lifted his shoulders and adjusted the lapels of his robe.

Jennie ignored the condescending tone in his voice. "As a matter of fact, I learned quite a lot."

She told him about the gunman in the llama pasture and seeing the truck at the Double D ranch.

"So, you've met Danielson." He pointed to the stump that used to be a leg and said, "Do you think he did this?"

Jennie sucked in a deep breath. "I—I don't know. Marty doesn't think so, but . . ."

He gripped the wheels of his chair and whirled it back around to face the window. "It's late. You'd better go to bed. We'll talk more tomorrow."

Jennie watched him for a few seconds. Tears gathered in her eyes and she didn't know why. One thing she did know. No matter what the odds, she had to find out who had maimed Jeff and taken Rick Jenkins' life. Sure, the truck she'd seen earlier in the day had been found, and the sheriff would question Danielson, but Jennie couldn't help but feel that she was seeing only a small piece of a much bigger and more complex puzzle.

Jennie and Heather reached the bedroom at the same time. One through the window, the other through the door. Jennie was beginning to wonder if Heather ever entered her room in the normal way.

"How's Eric?" Jennie asked.

Heather didn't answer.

"Your dad's downstairs waiting for you. He thought I was you when I first came in."

After closing the window, she turned to face Jennie. "Did you say anything about Eric?"

Jennie shook her head. "The subject didn't come up."

Heather sighed. "Guess I'd better go down and talk to him."

"What are you going to tell him?"

"The truth, I suppose. It's about time."

"Want me to come along?"

"No, but thanks for asking." Heather reached for the doorknob. "Wish me luck."

Jennie changed into a nightgown and went across the hall to the bathroom. She heard the murmur of voices downstairs and thought about sneaking over to the top of the stairs to eavesdrop, but didn't. Some conversations were meant to be private. Still, she couldn't help wonder how her uncle would react.

Ten minutes later Heather came in. Ignoring Jennie's questioning look, she entered the large walk-in closet, changed into her pajamas, then stood in front of the mirror and brushed out her shimmering black hair. After crawling under the covers, she turned out the light. "I didn't tell him."

Jennie rested her elbow on the pillow and propped her head up on her hand. "Why?"

"I just couldn't."

"So how did you explain your being out tonight?"

"I didn't," Heather murmured. "I said I was here all the time."

"And he believed you?"

"I don't know. He just sat there in the dark. He wouldn't even look at me. I let him down, Jen. Hazen and I . . ." Heather's voice broke into deep sobs.

Jennie got out of bed and retrieved a box of tissues from the dresser, handed a couple to Heather, then sat on the bed beside her. Heather blew her nose, then buried her face in the pillow.

Jennie placed what she hoped was a comforting hand on Heather's shoulder. After a few minutes, Heather's sobs quieted to an occasional shudder.

When it became apparent that Heather didn't want to talk anymore, Jennie climbed back into her own bed. She stared up into the darkness wishing she'd brought a tissue with her. Empathetic tears leaked out of the corners of her eyes and dripped into her hair and onto the pillow. She brushed them away with her hand. "Oh God," she whispered. "Why does life have to be so hard?" Jennie closed her eyes, squeezing out the last of her tears. She prayed for the fractured family, then for her own as her thoughts drifted back to home and Mom, Nick, Michael, and Hannah. She'd forgotten to call again. With the time difference they'd still be up. She thought about getting out of bed and going downstairs to the kitchen. No, Uncle Jeff might still be there. She didn't want to disturb him—or face him. Tomorrow. She'd call home tomorrow.

———

The next day when Jennie awoke, Heather had already gone to work. Jennie dressed as fast as her stiff muscles would allow and limped downstairs. Amber, Maggie, Jeff, and Bob

Lopez had already started to eat breakfast.

"Mornin', Jennie." Lopez speared a large piece of ham and plopped it onto his already full plate of pancakes and scrambled eggs.

"Good morning." Jennie pulled out the chair between him and Uncle Jeff's wheelchair and folded herself onto it. Her uncle offered her a brief nod, then turned back to his plate.

"Better eat hearty this mornin'," Lopez said. "You got a mighty big day ahead of you."

"Why's that?" Jennie reached for the eggs and gave Maggie a questioning look.

Maggie glanced at Jeff, then back at Jennie. "We thought you might enjoy working with Bob today. They'll be repairing the gate out in the llama pasture then checking out the herd." Her gaze fell to Jennie's cast. "Of course, you don't have to. I don't want you hurting that arm."

Jennie raised the arm in question. "Actually, it's not near as much problem as I thought it would be. I'm getting used to it. In fact, it's the only part of my body that doesn't hurt this morning. Anyway, I'd like to go."

"I'm going with," Amber said, sitting straighter in her chair.

"Not today." Jeff sipped at his coffee. "I'd like you to stick around here and keep your old dad company." His warm smile seemed like a contradiction to the man she'd met last night, but it made Jennie wish she could stay behind and get to know him better.

"If there's time," Jeff said, his gaze settling on Lopez, "I'd like you to ride on out to Dad's and check his stock. See if he needs anything."

Lopez nodded. "Heard they nailed Danielson last night."

"Yeah?" Jeff set his cup down, acting like he didn't know anything about it. Jennie wondered why.

"Seems his truck's the one what rammed our gate. Danielson swears up and down he wasn't driving it."

"He have any idea who was?"

"Claims not." Lopez shook his head. "Says his truck was stolen. Some story, huh? We all know how he feels about you and Joseph taking over the ranch."

"How'd you hear all this so quickly?" Jeff asked.

Lopez shrugged. "Danged if I know. Some of the boys was talking about it this morning—you know how word gets around."

Jennie set her fork down. Now she knew what her uncle was getting at. She hadn't told anyone but Jeff about the arrest. How would the ranch hands have found out so soon unless . . . Had one of them been there in the shadows, watching? If so, why? And who?

Or, her mind took another road, *maybe the person wasn't watching. Maybe they already knew because they'd stolen the pickup, returned it, and called the sheriff with the tip. That means the gunman and possibly the person who left the notes and killed the foreman could have been one of their own employees—or a member of the family.*

Jennie shivered at the possibility.

11

"I appreciate your taking me along, Mr. Lopez." Jennie eased Gabby up next to the ranch manager's horse as they rode out toward the llama pasture.

"Glad to have your company." Lopez shifted in his saddle and glanced at the brown truck lumbering up the hill behind them. It carried the supplies they'd need to build a new gate and mend the broken wire.

Jennie eyed the two men in the front seat—John Copeland and Eric Summers. She already had Eric on her list of suspects and wondered if she shouldn't include John, Heidi's husband. Heidi had been reluctant to talk about the problems at Dancing Waters.

Of course, she'd need to add Bob Lopez as well. She waited until he turned back around, then asked, "How long have you worked at the ranch?"

Lopez adjusted his hat and fixed his gaze on the brim. "Oh, reckon it's been 'bout twenty-five years or so. Started way back when your uncle Jeff was a young'n. Worked for the Elliots before that. When Dan Elliot moved the family to California, he let most of the hands go. Joseph asked me to stay on and work for him, and I've been here ever since."

"So you knew the Elliots. Joseph and Amber told me a little about them. Do you know Chad Elliot?"

"Seen him a couple of times. His daddy went west before

he was born. Met Chad when he showed up a few months back claiming his family had been swindled." He shook his head. "Crazy business, that."

"He didn't know his grandfather had sold off all the land to Joseph? I mean—that sounds so weird."

Lopez reached up and swatted at the fly buzzing around his head. "I wouldn't know about none of that. I just take care of the stock and the land. Leave the business to the bankers and the owners. Which reminds me—sure way to find out about the land deal would be to talk to Alex Dayton. He's president of the Bitterroot Valley Bank over in Cottonwood."

"Thanks. I might do that." She tucked the information away for future reference. "Do you think Joseph and Uncle Jeff cheated the Elliots out of their land?"

"Nope. Ain't nobody in Montana more honest than Joseph White Cloud. If he says the land is his, I believe him."

Jennie reached forward to stroke Gabby's neck. "Mr. Lopez, tell me about the explosion. Were you there? Do you think it was an accident?"

"You sure ask a lot of questions." Lopez pulled back on the reins to slow his mount until Jennie pulled up beside him. "You ain't planning on getting involved in the goings-on out here, are ya?"

"Well, I . . ."

"Now, I know you couldn't help what happened out here yesterday, but you want to be careful who yer askin' questions of."

"I am. I can trust you, can't I?"

A broad smile broke the solemn expression on his brown, furrowed face. "Reckon you can at that."

"So what about the explosion?"

He sighed, then as though indulging the whims of a child, "I wasn't out there that day. Had a touch of the flu. You know

I've felt real bad about it. Maybe if I'd been there I could have prevented it."

"Or you may have been the one who got killed." When he didn't respond, Jennie asked, "Do you think someone meant to murder the foreman?"

Lopez shook his head. "Reckon it must've been accidental. Can't think of a soul who'd want to kill Rick Jenkins. Poor guy had enough troubles. Trying to make ends meet—most folks just felt sorry for him. Wife had cancer—died not more'n two months before Rick was killed."

"Well, what if they weren't after him? What if they were after Uncle Jeff?"

Lopez shook his head. "Hmm, he's got plenty of enemies all right. Don't know anybody that hates him enough to want to kill him, though."

"Okay, then what if the explosion was just meant to scare the White Clouds into leaving? Maybe nobody was supposed to get hurt."

"I suppose that's a possibility."

Jennie knew she was pushing it, but had to ask one more question. "Do you think Jake Danielson did it?"

Lopez took a long time to answer. "I wouldn't put it past Danielson to come over and bag a deer or elk and maybe cut some wire, but setting off a bomb—that's not his style—leastwise it hasn't been. Course, having Joseph hand over half the land to the U.S. Forest Service has stirred up a mighty big hornet's nest. Lot of bad feeling over it, that's for sure."

"He's giving land to the government?"

Lopez gave her a long hard look. "No more questions now or I'll be tempted to tell your uncle what you're up to. I suspect he'll put an end to it right quick. We already got us a sheriff, Jennie. Might be better all around if you just let old Sam ask the questions. He'll be able to do something about the answers."

Lopez went on ahead, and when they reached the broken

fence, he reined up his quarter horse and dismounted. Jennie did too, or tried to. Her legs had stiffened again during the ride and when her feet hit the ground, her knees buckled. "Ouch." She grabbed at the saddle to straighten herself up.

Lopez chuckled. "A little sore, are ya?"

"A lot sore." Jennie winced as she shifted her weight from one foot to the other.

Lopez chuckled. "After all the riding you did yesterday, it's no wonder. You think yer bad off now, wait till tonight. We'd best get started. You hustle over to the truck and help the boys unload. With that arm, you might want to play gopher—just fetch and carry. Think you can handle that?"

"Sure. No problem." Some of the stiffness wore off as she worked. For the rest of the day, they mended fence in three different spots, checked on the llamas, the buffalo, and Joseph's Appaloosas. The white-and-brown horses had originally been bred and developed by the Nez Perce so they could easily identify members of their own tribe by the markings on their horses' rumps.

While working with the men, Jennie gleaned a little more information about Rick Jenkins. He'd not only been Danielson's buddy and a member of the militia, with his wife's medical bills, he'd been hurting for money. That information brought on a new pile of questions, but still left the big question unresolved. Had the explosion been intentional?

By the time Jennie arrived back at the ranch, had showered, and begun eating dinner, she could hardly lift the fork to her mouth. Even her brain hurt.

"Aren't you hungry?" Maggie asked.

Jennie gazed at the fried chicken, mashed potatoes and gravy, and string beans fresh out of the garden. "Starved. The stomach is willing, but my body just doesn't want to cooperate." With her left hand, she massaged the cramped muscles in her legs.

"We've been working you too hard."

"Wrong," Jeff teased as he lifted a piece of chicken to his mouth. "It's living in the city. She's not getting enough of the right kind of exercise. Another week around here, Jennie, and you'll be in great shape."

Jennie groaned. "If you don't kill me first."

"Poor baby," Heather cooed. "Mom, why don't I take her up to the Crystal Hot Springs after dinner? We can spend the night on Blue Ridge."

"Oh, Heather, how thoughtful." Maggie split open a hot buttermilk biscuit. "Jennie, you'll love it up there."

"Not a bad idea," Jeff said, "but first Maggie and I would like to talk to you in my study."

"Me?" Jennie glanced around the table.

Heather and Amber shrugged.

Maggie cleared her throat. "I . . . we . . . there's something we need to discuss with you."

For the rest of the meal Jennie's mind raced with possibilities. Was she in trouble? Had Lopez complained about her? Were they sending her home? Each question settled in her stomach like a rock.

"I'll pack and call Dusty to get the horses ready," Heather offered.

Something in her cousin's eyes raised the hair on Jennie's neck. Could she be planning something other than the trip? For a moment Jennie thought about telling her she'd do her own packing, but that would be rude. "Thanks," she said instead. "Be sure to put in a plastic bag to wrap my cast in so it doesn't get wet. I shouldn't be too long." *I hope.*

"Amber, honey . . ." Maggie picked up the leftover chicken and potatoes and carried them to the kitchen, "clear the table while Daddy and I talk to Jennie, okay? I'll be out to help you in a few minutes." Jennie tried not to stare at her uncle's legs as he backed away from the table. Before there'd been only one—now there were two.

"It's a prosthesis," he said, answering her question before she could ask it.

"Oh, I—um, I didn't mean to stare. I'm surprised, that's all. I didn't know they'd give you one so soon."

"They fitted me with it the day after surgery." Apparently not wanting to discuss his condition further, he propelled his wheelchair toward the office.

"Sit down, Jennie." Jeff wheeled the chair behind his desk.

Jennie sat in one of the two forest green armchairs and glanced over the two walls of books. It looked like an office you'd expect a lawyer to have.

Maggie stood behind her and rested her hands on Jennie's shoulders.

"Okay, I give. What did I do wrong?"

"Wrong?" Jeff frowned then looked up at Maggie.

Maggie squeezed Jennie's shoulders. "You haven't done anything wrong. It's just that your mother called earlier and we thought it would be better to talk privately."

"Mom? Oh no. It's Hannah, isn't it? They couldn't get her back. I knew it. I should have gone home. . . ."

"There was nothing they could do." Jeff placed his elbows on his desk, locked his fingers together, and rested his chin on his hands. "Nothing you could do, either. Hannah's grandparents have exercised their right to care for Hannah. The judge granted them custody."

"But Chuck Stewart is a . . ." Jennie groped for a word but couldn't think of anything bad enough to describe him.

"Apparently he's never abused Hannah," Jeff went on. "She won't be living with him—at least not right away. He will have visitation rights, and may eventually gain custody, but for now, Mr. and Mrs. Stewart will be responsible for her. The court feels it's in Hannah's best interest to be with her biological family."

Jennie bit her lower lip, not bothering to wipe away the

tears that had broken loose. "It's not fair. Isn't there anything they could have done?"

"I'm afraid not, honey." Maggie covered Jennie's hand with her own. "Jeff says they can appeal, but Susan—um, your mother thinks it may be less disruptive for Hannah to let her go."

"How can she. . . ?" Jennie brushed the moisture off her cheeks with her palms. "I'd better call her."

Jeff wheeled his chair around the desk and pulled up next to the door. "I wish you could call her. To tell you the truth, the last thing I need to deal with right now is another problem."

"Jeff . . ." Maggie began.

Her uncle grabbed the doorknob, then turned back and sighed. "I'm sorry. I had no right to take my frustrations out on you."

"It's okay, Uncle Jeff. Why can't I call Mom?"

"She's on her way to Arizona with Michael and Nick." Maggie squeezed Jennie's hand.

"Arizona? What are they doing in Arizona? They're supposed to be coming here."

"They'll be here in a few days. Susan wanted to ease the transition for Hannah and check out her grandparents."

The thought of never seeing Hannah again dug a crater in Jennie's heart. She pressed the heels of her hands against her eyes. "How could Mom and Michael give up so easily?"

"Oh, honey." Maggie drew Jennie into her arms. "I know it's hard. But Susan said to tell you that Hannah's grandparents seem very nice."

"Think of it this way, Jennie," Jeff said. "Suppose you were in Hannah's place. Would you rather live with your neighbors or with your grandparents?"

Jennie raised her head. "I—when you put it that way—but . . ." She released a long, shuddering sigh. "Do you think she's really better off?"

"Only time will tell. Hannah's grandparents want you and your family to stay in touch. You can write and even visit."

"Really?"

"Yes. Since you didn't get to say good-bye to Hannah, you can fly down later this summer."

The thought of seeing Hannah for herself took the edge off the pain.

Jeff wheeled back to his desk again and picked up a folder. Maggie hugged Jennie and excused herself to go help Amber in the kitchen.

Jennie started to follow, then stopped at the door. "Uncle Jeff?" A nagging question had re-inserted itself in her mind and she had to ask.

He looked up from his papers. "Yes?"

"Can you tell me about the explosion?"

12

"I mean . . . was the explosion an accident or. . . ?" Jennie hesitated. Maybe he didn't want to talk about it yet.

"Did someone blow up the truck on purpose?" Jeff finished. He stared at something on his desk for a long time, then closed his eyes. "I wish I knew. The truth is, I can't remember. I close my eyes and all I can see is the explosion and the flames. Nothing more."

Jennie walked over to her uncle's desk. "Did you know about the death threats Heather and Joseph got while you were gone?"

"My father told me of the message left on the deer." He raised an eyebrow. "And how you took the note from his garbage."

Jennie's cheeks flushed. "I . . . he threw it away and I thought it might be important. Monday—the day I arrived—Heather and I had stopped for lunch and when we came out of the restaurant there was a note on the Jeep. They were written by the same person." She pulled the papers from her pocket to show him.

"Why didn't you give them to the sheriff?"

"I probably should have last night when he was over at the Danielsons, but I forgot. Actually, that's not entirely true. Maybe I didn't really forget. Heather said she didn't trust him. I wasn't too impressed with him either."

"Might be just as well, in case we have to go to another law enforcement agency. He let Danielson go," Jeff said, his voice flat and without the anger she expected.

"On bail?"

"Sam didn't arrest him."

"I can't believe that. Look at the evidence."

"He did. His deputies weren't able to lift any fingerprints from the interior of the truck, which means it had been wiped clean. He figures Danielson would have no reason to do that. There's nothing to indicate who drove it. What's more, Sam would need absolute proof to arrest Jake. The man's his brother-in-law and practically owns him."

"So you're saying that even if Danielson is guilty, he won't be arrested?"

"Not without infallible evidence, with eyewitnesses to testify against him. I should amend that to honest witnesses."

Jennie stared at her uncle. She wasn't sure how to respond. She placed her left arm on Jeff's desk and leaned toward him. "I don't get it. How come you're telling me all this? How come you're not shoving me out to play and telling me to mind my own business?"

"I don't trust Sam Mason. He's too easily swayed by special interest groups. Though he won't admit it, he's sympathetic to the white supremacists and anti-government groups and as far as I'm concerned that's a dangerous place to be. If I could be out there solving this case I would."

He paused and glanced down at his leg. "But I can't—leastwise not yet. I'd planned to tell you tomorrow when you came back from Blue Ridge, but I guess now is as good a time as any." He paused and held her in a long steady gaze. "I need someone to investigate for me."

Stunned, Jennie moved over to the chair and dropped into it. "You want me to . . . investigate?"

Jeff smiled. "Trust me, Jennie. If it were solely up to me, you would not be my first choice. Not that you aren't competent. But you are my sister-in-law's kid. If Maggie or Susan find out I've encouraged you, I'd be . . . well let's just say I'd rather you didn't tell either of them we're having this discussion."

"I don't get it."

"I spoke with my father today. He believes God has sent you to help us. He says that you are going to investigate with or without our blessing and, considering this, feels we should assist you. At the moment I'm not so sure. But my father is a wise man. I'm willing to support his decision, but you'll need to report everything you learn to me. If I'm not here you must speak with my father."

"Are you serious? You actually want me to investigate?"

Jeff nodded. "I'm afraid so. There's one more thing. Be careful. Don't go off alone with Marty Danielson or any of the other men around here. Don't even trust the sheriff. Snooping around and digging up information is one thing. I doubt any of these men will be taking you seriously, which gives us the advantage. Joseph and I will be watching out for you as best we can. So will Bob."

"He knows?"

"He came in to talk to me before dinner. Said you were asking all kinds of questions." Jeff grinned. "Don't worry, you can trust him. Bob Lopez is like a second father to me."

"Thanks, Uncle Jeff." Jennie bounced out of her chair, walked around the desk, and threw her arms around his neck. When the cast connected with his head she mumbled an apology and backed away. "Sorry."

"No problem."

"I guess I'd better go."

As she reached the door, Jeff stopped her. "There's one more thing, Jennie. If you happen to find Hazen—" His eyes closed and he frowned. "Just tell him I don't hold him responsible for anything that happened out there."

"What makes you think I'll see him?"

Jeff shook his head. "Wishful thinking, I guess. That and your track record."

Still stunned, Jennie left. Except for Gram he'd been the only adult to take her seriously. Excitement bubbled up inside her, then ebbed. *What if you fail, McGrady? What if you let them down? And who are you to take on a case like this? You're dealing with a militia group, not the Boy Scouts.*

"Come on, Jennie. I've got everything all ready." Heather stuffed a swimsuit into Jennie's hand a pushed her out of Jeff's office and in the direction of the main floor bathroom. As instructed, Jennie put the swimsuit on under her clothes.

When Jennie emerged, Heather led her out to the front porch where she'd set their boots. "You're going to love the surprise I have planned for you."

"What surprise?" Jennie sat on the steps beside Heather and pulled on her boots. "You said you were taking me to some hot springs, then camping on Blue Ridge. Is there more?"

"Definitely, but I can't tell you." Heather flashed her an infectious smile.

"I can hardly wait." Jennie set aside the warning bells and decided her cousin had gone through an attitude change. After all, they had grown closer in the last couple of days. Maybe Heather had decided they could be friends. Maybe.

Heather scrambled to her feet and reached down to give Jennie a hand up. The fast movement set off a chain reaction in her sore muscles. "Whoa. Take it easy."

"Sorry."

Mounting Gabby should have been getting easier, but Jennie's legs and hips protested more loudly with each try. "Ouch. I may have to give up riding if this gets any worse."

"Another day or two and you'll be fine." Heather turned her honey-colored mare named Brandy and headed southwest down the same path she'd taken on the night Jennie had gotten lost. The thought didn't exactly fill Jennie with confidence.

The deeper into the woods they rode, the stronger Jennie's suspicions grew. Heather chatted about her last photo shoot with Eric. "I am so excited, Jennie. His agent has me scheduled to do a photo session with Andre."

"Who's Andre?" Jennie asked.

"Only the most popular photographer on the West Coast. His photos have been on the cover of every major magazine in the country this year. And nearly all of his models are doing films. This is a major break for me."

"So, when is all this supposed to happen?" Jennie asked.

"You sound like you don't believe me."

"Oh, I believe *you*. It's Eric I'm worried about."

"Eric loves me. He wouldn't lie about something this important. It's our dream."

"When are you going to tell your folks?"

"I'm not. Well, I did leave them a note, but . . ."

"What do you mean, you left them a note?" Jennie's loud response startled Gabby. The horse shied, nearly dumping her on the trail. She grasped the saddle horn and held on tight.

"Whoa, Gabby. It's okay. I'm sorry." She patted Gabby's neck and glared at Heather. "Well?"

Heather stared back, unflinching. "I have to do this. I may never get another opportunity. My parents won't understand."

"All right. Go ahead. Mess up your life. But don't expect me to help you. I'm going back to the ranch." Jennie winced. She was beginning to sound like her mother.

"You're not going to tell, are you?"

"Yes . . . I don't know. I should. You could be setting yourself up for . . . anything. I've heard some pretty gruesome stories about girls who run away from home wanting to be models or actresses. They leave home expecting a career and end up living on the street."

"That's not going to happen."

"I hope not. What you're doing is dangerous."

"I thought maybe you'd understand. You can go back to the ranch, but even if you tell Mom and Dad it won't do any good. I'm going." Heather spurred her horse forward.

Jennie debated. Should she go back or stay with Heather? If she stayed, maybe she'd be able to talk her out of leaving.

"Okay, I give. I'll come with you. I won't tell your parents—yet. Just explain one thing. If you were going to run away, why drag me into it?"

"I wasn't dragging you in. Actually, I'm not leaving until tomorrow. I just wanted to share my good news and spend some time with you before I leave." Heather smiled. "It's hard to know when we'll get together again and I'm starting to like you."

Jennie wanted to believe her, but her intuition cautioned her to tread carefully.

A few minutes later, they emerged from the trees and rode along a ridge.

"We'll be there soon. Can you hear the waterfall?"

The rushing sound of water eased Jennie's nerves. Maybe Heather was just taking her to the hot springs. They rode on in silence for several minutes, then entered the woods again and rode until they came to a wide meadow divided by a creek.

The creek gave rise to a steep rock formation where water dropped from a hundred-foot cliff. Beside the waterfall, steam rose from an almost circular pool.

"Oh . . . Oh, Heather," Jennie whispered. "It's beautiful."

"I told you. Wait until you get in."

The girls tied their horses to a nearby tree, stripped down to their swimming suits, and set their towels on the rocks. Heather climbed in while Jennie sat on the edge and wrapped her cast in plastic wrap. She eased her body into the pool, taking care to keep the cast out of the water. Her aching muscles soon began to relax as the warm water melted away her tension.

"I've been thinking about what you said." Heather tipped her head back and gazed at the colorful western sky.

"About what?" The water had relaxed her so much Jennie had let their discussion about Eric float away. Now it drifted back. "Oh, you mean about running away?"

"You might be right. I mean, I do trust Eric, but I don't know anything about the agent. I may not show it sometimes, but I love my family. I wouldn't want to hurt them." Heather shifted her gaze from the pink and lavender sky to Jennie. "Do you think Mom and Dad would let me go?"

Jennie shrugged. "I don't know. They might say no, but if your folks are anything like my mom, they'd have a good reason."

"I don't think I could bear it if they said no."

"I sort of understand where you're coming from. I want to go into law enforcement—maybe become a detective or a police officer. Mom thinks being a lawyer is okay, but says the other is too dangerous. I figure I'll just give her some time to get used to the idea, go to college, then decide for sure. The one thing I know is that whatever choice I make, Mom will be there for me."

"Hmm. Maybe I will talk to them."

"They might surprise you."

Heather slid beneath the water again, her jet black hair splayed out on the water as she ducked under. She popped up laughing and splashing.

"Hey, no fair. I can't get all the way in." Jennie reciprocated by kicking up a wall of water. Heather called a truce.

"Look," Heather said, pointing up at the dusky sky. "The first star. Do you ever wish on it?"

Jennie nodded. "I used to wish I'd find my father. I

haven't made a wish for a long time."

"Star light, star bright, first star I see tonight. I wish I may, I wish I might, have the wish I wish tonight." Heather squeezed her eyes tight.

Jennie did the same. She wished for Heather to make the right choice. And for Hazen to come home. And for Hannah to be safe and well. "I have too many things to wish for."

"Me too." Heather sighed.

When they climbed out of the hot springs, the darkening sky had turned the stars to diamonds. After removing their wet suits, they toweled dry and dragged on their clothes. Jennie was amazed at how clearly she could see with only the moon for a night-light.

As Jennie slipped on a sweatshirt the hairs on the back of her head sprang to attention. She glanced around. "Heather?"

No one answered. Jennie walked around the rocks to where they'd left the horses. They were gone.

Oh no, not again. "Come on, Heather, this isn't funny."

An eerie silence bred fear in her heart. "Heather?"

A coyote howled an answer in the distance. Jennie shivered as she scanned the moonlit hills. Shadows. Too many shadows.

A twig snapped. Jennie whirled around. Not more than fifteen feet in front of her—astride a huge silver-white horse—sat an Indian warrior. Long black hair shimmered in the moonlight and streamed behind him as the wind sliced through the canyon. He stared at her with eyes dark as the night.

Jennie backed up against a rock. This couldn't be real. She half expected a director to walk on stage and tell her she was playing the scene all wrong. "Who—who are you?"

The warrior didn't answer. His menacing gaze fastened on her. Jennie thought about running, but couldn't move. He lifted a hatchet from his belt, raised it high above his head, and hurled it toward her.

13

"Is she all right?" The voice belonged to Heather.

Jennie gritted her teeth. *You should have known, McGrady.
You should have seen it coming.*

"You think the tomahawk was too much?" The second
voice was male. If he hadn't frightened her out of her wits
she might have recognized him.

Jennie got to her knees, ignoring Hazen's offer of help.
Like Heather, he had coal black hair and wide, dark eyes.
Glistening white teeth appeared as he grinned at her. "Hi,
Jennie. Welcome to Dancing Waters."

Jennie brushed herself off. Fury wiped away any fear
she'd felt earlier. "I can't believe you'd trick me like that."

"Why?" they answered in unison.

Jennie shook her head. "You nearly gave me a heart attack. You could have killed me."

"Not a chance." Hazen jumped up on the rock and retrieved his tomahawk from a tree stump. "I missed you by at
least two feet."

"Don't be mad at us, Jennie. It's my fault. I knew you
wanted to meet Hazen and I thought this would be fun."

Jennie huffed. "Getting a hatchet tossed at me is not my
idea of fun."

"Well, you have to admit we had you going." Hazen
chuckled as he snapped his tomahawk back onto his belt. He
reached toward her head.

Jennie flinched. "What are you doing?"

"Hold still." He pulled a twig out of her hair. "You're a mess."

"Thanks," Jennie muttered as she brushed the dirt off her hands and clothes.

"Let's go back in the water for a while," Heather suggested. "You need to wash off the dirt."

Jennie didn't argue and was, in fact, the first one in. The warm water worked its magic and after a while she could almost laugh at the practical joke her cousins had played on her. They talked for another half hour, then headed back to their horses.

"I hope this means we're forgiven, Jennie." Hazen draped one arm around Jennie's shoulders and the other around his sister.

"Are we really staying out here tonight?" Jennie asked, "or are we heading back to the ranch?"

"That's up to you." Heather swung up onto Brandy's back. "I'm staying out here. I think Hazen is too, but, if you want, we can escort you to the house, then come back out."

"No, don't do that. I'll stay, but no more practical jokes."

It took all of five minutes to make the trek to the one-room cabin that sat alone on Blue Ridge. The stars and moon hung so near, Jennie could almost touch them. Hazen built a fire in a pit near the cabin to chase away the mountain chill while Heather and Jennie cut branches for roasting marshmallows. They feasted on s'mores, chocolate bars and smooshed hot marshmallows sandwiched between two Graham crackers.

Around midnight, they pulled sleeping bags from the cabin and placed them out under the big Montana sky. Jennie snuggled into her bag. She'd never seen so many stars or been able to make out so many constellations. After a while her eyes drifted closed. Then she remembered what her uncle Jeff had said. "Hazen?" she whispered.

"What?" He raised up on his elbow.

"Your dad sent a message for you."

Hazen lowered his head to the pillow. "Do I want to hear this?"

"He doesn't hold you responsible for what happened."

After a long silence, Jennie turned onto her side facing him. "Why did you run away?"

Hazen glanced over at Heather, then unzipped his bag and crawled out. "She's asleep. Let's talk over there."

Jennie scrambled out of her bag and followed him to the other side of the cabin. He sat on an outcropping of rock and waited for Jennie to join him.

"My father is wrong," Hazen said. "It was my fault. I knew Rick was planning something. I'd seen him talking to Danielson a couple of days before. I should have told Dad, but I thought I'd just keep an eye on him myself."

"You think Rick caused the explosion?"

"I know he did. My guess is he was working for Danielson. I saw him toss something into the fuel tank. He took off running. Tripped on a rock. Section of tailgate caught him in the back."

"Oh, Hazen. How awful."

"Dad was supposed to die. Rick had waited until he thought I was out of sight. Only I'd forgotten a wire cutter and was riding back."

"I don't understand why you'd blame yourself."

"I was scared. All that blood . . . and my dad's leg. I tried to stop the bleeding. Took Dad to the hospital, but I couldn't stay. If I'd warned him about Rick, he might have fired the guy." Hazen lowered his head to his knees.

"You don't know that." Jennie placed her hand on his arm. "It's not your fault. If the explosion hadn't injured your father, the militia—or whoever is responsible—would have tried again. Come back to the ranch with me tomorrow. Your folks really want to see you—Amber too."

Hazen nodded. "I'll think about it."

As shades of dawn crept over the hills, Jennie awoke to the sound of horses' hooves and voices. She snuggled deeper inside the bag. A few minutes later the silence, not voices, brought her more fully awake. She stretched and rubbed her eyes, then eased out of her sleeping bag. The two bags that had been laid out next to her were gone. "Not again." Jennie was growing weary of the twins' idea of fun. She rolled up her bag, set it on the cabin steps, and went in search of Gabby. They'd tied the horses to some trees nearby, but now Jennie saw no sign of them or of her companions.

"Wonderful. I suppose they expect me to walk back." Jennie picked up her sleeping bag and banged open the door to the cabin. She groped along the wall for a light switch, and when she found it, flipped it on. Jennie tossed the sleeping bag on one of the six bunks and paced the floor. Her fury increased with each step. She stopped abruptly. Pacing and getting mad wasn't going to solve the problem.

At least they hadn't left her without food. The night before they'd told her the cabin was always well stocked. Jennie rummaged through the small refrigerator and pantry and before long the scent of bacon and eggs permeated the air.

A horse whinnied only moments before the door swung open. Hazen offered her a wide smile as he stepped inside. "Smells good. Make enough for me?" He'd exchanged his warrior look for jeans, western boots, and a forest green Dancing Waters Sweatshirt.

"You can have this. I'll make some more." Jennie scooped up a forkful of bacon and set it on paper towels to drain, then dished up the eggs. "I thought you'd gone. I was going to eat breakfast, then try to find my way back to the ranch."

Hazen came up behind her and grabbed a slice of bacon. "You thought we'd leave you out here alone?"

"You tossed a hatchet at me."

"Not at you. At a tree stump."

"What happened to the horses?"

"I took them down to the creek."

"Where's Heather?" Jennie finished dishing up a plate and handed it to him.

He carried it to the rustic wooden table and straddled the bench. "Gone."

"She went with Eric? I thought maybe she'd changed her mind." Jennie broke two eggs into a bowl and whisked them a bit harder than necessary, then poured them into the hot frying pan.

"Me too. I tried to talk her out of it." He shoveled a forkful of eggs into his mouth. "Maybe she'll still change her mind."

Jennie watched the eggs set, turning them with the spatula. "Why did she even bring me out here? Never mind. I think I know. She wanted to make it look like she was out camping with me so your parents wouldn't suspect."

"Don't be too angry with her, Jennie."

"Why not? She's been using me ever since I got here. First she keeps me waiting for hours at the airport so she can play kissy face with her boyfriend, then she makes up with me so I won't tell on her when she sneaks out in the middle of the night." Jennie piled the eggs and bacon on her plate, took it to the table, and began eating.

"I'm sorry." Hazen watched her eat and Jennie watched the sky outside the window lighten to a pale blue.

"Why do you keep looking at me like that?"

"I am amazed at how much we look alike. Your hair and eyes are so dark, yet you have no Indian blood."

She let her gaze latch onto his and frowned. "Your hair is darker."

"Not much. Our eyes are the same."

Jennie leaned closer. She hadn't noticed it before, but his were different from Heather's—more navy than violet.

A grin spilt his handsome bronzed face. "We could be twins."

"Speaking of twins, shouldn't we try to stop yours?" Jennie asked, changing the subject. "I mean, they can't have gone too far."

"No. This modeling thing is important to Heather. It may not be the right decision, but she needs to be the one to make it."

"I'll tell you one thing, I'm not looking forward to breaking the news to your parents."

Hazen shook his head. "Me either. I'm afraid Heather and I have been a great disappointment to them. This past year has been hard for all of us."

After breakfast, Jennie and Hazen cleaned up the dishes, then rode back to the ranch. During the hour-long ride, Hazen shared his struggles over the last few years in trying to balance his two vastly different cultures.

"Why has it been so hard for you? I think it would be neat to be part Indian."

"I am learning to be proud of my heritage now. Joseph is helping me to understand my people. For a long time I have felt like a man trapped between two worlds. I thought I had to choose between the two."

"Why would you have to choose? I mean, couldn't you just be yourself?"

Hazen chuckled. "It seems simple enough now. Heather has always been able to do that—and Amber. But not me. Mom always accuses me of doing things the hard way."

As they broke through the trees and came within view of the ranch, Hazen reined in his horse, an Appaloosa named Thunder. He closed his eyes and took a deep breath as if to brace himself for the storm ahead. And there would be one. Even though neither of them could have stopped Heather from leaving, both would be blamed.

"Well, this is it." He dug his heels into Thunder's sides.

They didn't slow down until they reached the house. Amber, Maggie, and Jeff were still seated at the breakfast table when Jennie and Hazen walked in.

"Hazen!" Amber bounced out of the chair and ran into his arms.

He lifted her up and spun her around. "Hey, Short Stuff. Did you miss me?"

"You shouldn't have gone away," Amber scolded.

"I know." When Hazen tried to lower her to the floor, Amber buried her face in his neck and held on tight. He gave up and carried her to the table.

Maggie pushed her chair back and, for a moment, Jennie thought she'd rush over to embrace Hazen as well, but Uncle Jeff gave her a hard look that seemed to freeze her in place. He shifted that look to Hazen. Were they going to argue?

"Your grandfather's stock needs looking after," Jeff said. "He's got a mare ready to foal. Could use your help out there today."

Hazen nodded. Jennie could almost feel his tension drain out along with her own. He unhooked Amber's arms from his neck and set her on her chair next to his.

"Where's Heather?" Jeff asked.

Hazen's gaze met Jennie's. "She's . . ."

"Jeff! Maggie!" The back door swung open and Lopez strode into the dining room. "You'd better come down to the stables quick. One of the hands just came in with a gunshot wound."

Maggie jumped to her feet. "Oh no. Who is it? What happened?"

"Don't know how or why, but it's that new guy you hired, Eric Summers. Somebody shot him."

14

If Eric's been shot, what happened to Heather? Jennie jumped to her feet, ran out the door, and leaped onto Gabby's back. Hazen followed with Thunder as they raced down to the stables. In one fluid motion, Hazen dismounted and ran into the barn with Jennie at his heels. A siren split the air as they reached the couch in Dusty's office where Eric now lay.

"Heather's pony brought him in," Dusty shifted to one side as Hazen dropped to one knee beside Eric.

"The bleeding's pretty well stopped, but I can't seem to rouse him."

Jennie hunkered down beside Hazen and pressed her fingers against Eric's neck. His face was pasty white, his lips blue. He'd been shot in the shoulder. Blood soaked a quarter of his shirt, seeping into his shirt pocket.

"I can feel a pulse, but it's weak." She rose and backed away to make room for the paramedics.

Hazen scrambled to his feet, plowed past the two men from the rescue unit. Jennie followed him out of the office to where they'd left the horses. He vaulted onto Thunder's back and raced away.

"Hazen, wait!" Jennie yelled into the dust kicked up by the horse's hooves. She reached for Gabby, then looked back at her uncle and Lopez who were making their way toward her.

Jeff's eyes narrowed as he stared after his son. "Let him go. Boy's running away from everything these days."

"It's not what you think. He's not running away. I think he's gone to find Heather. Whoever shot Eric . . ." Jennie stopped and sighed. "It's a long story."

Twenty minutes later, when the ambulance was gone and they'd all gathered back in Dusty's office, Jennie told her story to Sheriff Mason, Jeff, Lopez, and Maggie. She began by explaining the relationship between Heather and Eric. "Heather had been sneaking out to meet him and they were planning to go to California. Hazen and I tried to talk her out of it, but she was gone when I woke up this morning."

"Where was she supposed to meet him?" Jeff asked.

"She didn't say."

The sheriff straightened and, with a look on his face that accused her of lying, said, "Well now, little lady, that was quite a story." He brought a plastic bag out of his jacket pocket containing a blood-stained piece of paper. "We found this note in the boy's pocket. I've bagged it—want to check for prints, though I doubt we'll find any. Apparently your little girl's been kidnapped."

"What?" they chorused.

"Let me see it." Jeff reached for the bagged note.

The sheriff handed it to him. "I'll need to keep it as evidence."

"What does it say?" Jennie asked.

Jeff handed the plastic-protected note to her. On a pale green shade of paper she'd seen too many times before, someone had scrawled, *You'll see your daughter as soon as you deed Dancing Waters back over to its rightful owner.*

Jeff shook his head. "I can't believe Elliot would do something so stupid."

"Does seem strange he'd draw attention to himself that way, but you never know." Mason took back the bag and pocketed it. "I'll go on into town and have a talk with him—

that is if he's still around. Any idea where he might be staying?"

Jeff rubbed his forehead. "No. Greg Bennett should know. You might want to call him anyway. He'll want to know what his client's been up to."

Lopez lifted the brim of his hat with a forefinger, then let it drop back onto his head. "I might know where to find Elliot. Saw him a couple of days ago heading into Marsha's Bed & Breakfast. Only I don't reckon he's the one you're lookin' for. Chad Elliot don't seem like the type of man . . ."

"You've talked to him?" Jeff snapped.

"He . . . ah . . . called me when he first got to town. I reckon I should have told you."

"I reckon so." Jeff's jaw had gone rigid and Jennie wondered if the ranch manager's rendezvous with the enemy would get him fired. "We'll talk about this later."

Lopez rubbed a hand across his face. "Like I was saying, Elliot didn't seem like the kind that'd resort to kidnapping. He thinks he's got a good case—no sense jeopardizing that. I reckon Danielson's behind this. He'll do anything to keep Dancin' Waters from being signed over to the Forestry Service. He glared at Sheriff Mason. "If you'd a put him in jail this wouldn't have happened."

Sheriff Mason shot Lopez a disgusted look. "Not that I owe you any explanations, but we didn't have enough evidence against Jake to arrest him. He wouldn't have done something like this anyway. He's got a kid of his own."

Jeff clasped his hands together on his lap. "Look, Mason, I know you and I are at opposite ends of the poles politically, but—"

"What kind of man do you think I am, White Cloud? You think I'd let political differences interfere with upholding the law?" He started to leave, then turned back around at the door. "I've already got deputies at work on this. We'll find her."

He left then, but the tension in the room increased as Bob Lopez and Jeff White Cloud eyed each other like two bull moose laying claim to their territory. Lopez's confession, if that's what it was, called his character into question. He'd spoken with Chad Elliot. Could he also be conspiring with him against the White Clouds? He'd originally worked for the Elliots. Had Chad Elliot bought him back? The look on Jeff's face told Jennie he was wondering the same thing.

"I'm going to get back to work." Maggie released her white-knuckled hold on Jeff's chair. "The ranch isn't going to run itself."

Jeff reached up and squeezed Maggie's hand. "I'd better call Dad. Then I suspect I'll have to call Alex to get the papers ready just in case."

Maggie bent to kiss him, then straightened. "Jennie, come with me please."

Jennie followed Maggie out of the office and occasionally glanced at her aunt as they walked. Maggie reminded her more of Mom every day. She wished she could tell Maggie everything would be all right, but Jennie had no idea how things would turn out. "Aunt Maggie, I—I'm sorry about Heather. Hazen and I both tried to talk her out of going with Eric. Now—"

"Don't blame yourself, Jennie. If someone wanted to kidnap Heather they'd have done it regardless of whether or not she planned to leave. I wish we'd taken this modeling business more seriously. I just hope it's not too late."

Jennie didn't know what to say, so she settled for a hug. When they reached the steps of the main lodge, Maggie leaned against one of the thick logs on either side of the wide steps. "I'd like you to watch Amber for me today. I don't want her to be alone."

Jennie nodded. "I'll be happy to watch her."

"Um—if she gets too rambunctious you can take her down to the stables and ride in the arena, and maybe go swimming in the guest pool, but stay on the grounds. While you're in the house be sure you keep the doors locked."

Jennie nodded again. "I will."

"She's with Heidi right now. I'll need to tell her about Heather."

"We'll tell her together," Jeff said as he and Lopez approached them.

Lopez pushed the wheelchair up the ramp next to the lodge steps. "I'd best be going. I'll check in with you every hour or so." The ranch mananger tipped his hat, and left. Apparently they'd resolved their differences—at least for the time being.

"I'll call the house and have Heidi bring Amber down." Jeff grabbed the wheels and propelled himself into the lodge office.

Amber didn't say much when Jeff and Maggie told her about Heather and Eric. After they'd talked about it and reassured her, Amber's intense gaze drilled into her parents. "You're not giving up the ranch, are you?"

Maggie and Jeff looked at each other, then back at Amber. "I don't know," Jeff answered. "Amber—honey—no matter what happens, we'll be together as a family."

After a light lunch, Jennie and Amber left the lodge. "You girls be careful." Maggie hugged Amber for the tenth time. She and Jeff watched from the porch as Jennie pulled Amber down the steps. Deep furrows lined their foreheads.

"Let's exercise the horses," Amber suggested, turning toward the stables.

"Sure." Jennie remembered what Amber had said about how riding made her feel better. "I could use another lesson."

Alex Dayton pulled into the driveway, spraying gravel as he ground to a stop. He jumped out and jogged toward them, his tie flapping against his expensive black suit. "Have you heard anything?" he panted.

"No. Just the note so far," Jeff answered.

"I am so sorry about Heather. If there's anything I can do . . ."

"Thanks, Alex. We appreciate that."

Dayton's sky-blue gaze drifted from Jeff to Jennie and Amber. He reached down and ruffled Amber's hair. "How's the little Sunshine?"

Amber pulled back and adjusted her curls. "I'm mad."

Maggie gave Amber a behave-yourself look.

He shifted his attention to Jennie. "I've seen you around a couple of times, but I don't believe we've officially met. I'm Alex Dayton."

"I'm sorry," Maggie said. "I should have introduced you yesterday. Alex and his dad own most of the banks around these parts. He's been about the only friend that's stuck by us since all this land business started."

"Hi," Jennie replied.

Alex Dayton gave her a warm smile and a nod. "The pleasure's mine." He turned back to the adults, climbed up the steps, and stopped in front of Jeff. "I brought the information you wanted. Wish I could talk you out of it, but I suppose this is the best way. Let's just hope Sheriff Mason is able to find Heather. I know I shouldn't be breaking confidences, but I talked to Greg. He's hopping mad. Says he's wondering if Elliot and Danielson are in on it together. He's about ready to drop Elliot's case."

Jeff reached for the thick envelope Dayton held.

Dayton ran well-manicured fingers through his thinning blond hair. "There must be some other way, Jeff. Giving in to the kidnapper's demands just doesn't seem right."

"If you think of one, let us know." Uncle Jeff spun the chair around. "Let's talk in the office."

Jennie felt sick. She couldn't believe they'd give up Dancing Waters. "Come on, Amber. Let's go."

"We gotta do something to stop them, Jennie." Amber's eyes had changed, misted. "We just have to."

Jennie squeezed her cousin's hand, groping for the right words. None came.

They'd worked the horses for twenty minutes when Amber announced she wanted to go swimming. Jennie agreed and followed Amber out of the arena into the stables. Without waiting for Amber, Jennie swung off Gabby and came around to pet his forehead. "You are such a good horse. I could ride you all day."

Gabby snorted and snuffled at her shoulder. "How are you doing, Amber? Ready to help me with the saddle?" Jennie might have been able to manage the saddle alone but didn't want to take the chance of dropping it.

When Amber didn't answer, Jennie glanced toward Cinnamon's stall across the way. Amber wasn't there. She heard the clip-clop of hooves at the far end of the stable, then caught a glimpse of a red-brown rump and black tail as Cinnamon disappeared out the door.

"Uh-oh." Jennie pulled Gabby away from his stall and got back into the saddle. "I don't know what she thinks she's doing, but I have a feeling it's not good." She snapped the reins and urged the gelding forward. The horse trotted out the door and across the pasture. Jennie spotted Amber as she and Cinnamon jumped the fence. She groaned. Dusty came around the corner. He'd seen Amber too and started running after her.

"I'll get her," Jennie yelled. *Or die trying.*

Jennie stopped breathing before they reached the fence. She looped the reins around her wrist and held tight to the saddle horn, leaving her right arm free and waving in the air to help maintain her balance. A lesson or two on jumping might have been nice. She closed her eyes as Gabby's front hooves left the ground. *Please make it. Please.*

Her eyes flew open as Gabby's hooves hit the ground. He'd apparently done this before. The gelding galloped on, following Amber and Cinnamon into the woods.

The gray overcast sky grew darker as it started to rain.

Jennie caught up to Amber at the llama pasture, where she'd stopped to open the gate. "I'm surprised you didn't try to jump this one too," Jennie snapped.

"She could slip in the mud and get cut on the barbed wire. 'Sides, I didn't think you'd catch up to me so fast." Amber led Cinnamon through the gate and waited for Jennie. Rain had plastered her red-gold hair against her head. "I'm going to see Papa and you can't stop me."

"I could, but I won't." Jennie rode Gabby through, not bothering to get down. If Amber wanted to run off on her own, she could deal with the gate herself. Besides, she wasn't about to let Amber out of her sight again. "Your folks are probably worried sick by now." She paused to button her denim jacket, then turned up the collar to keep the water from dripping down her neck.

Amber pouted. "I don't care. I have to talk to Papa. He'll know what to do."

Maybe he would. At least there they'd be safe and dry. "Since we're closer to his place, we'll go to your grandfather's and call your folks." What worried Jennie was getting to Joseph's house. It was still a long way. The rain had grown into a relentless downpour.

Jennie let out a long sigh of relief when they finally rode into Joseph's yard, past his Ford Ranger, and up to the porch. They dismounted, tied the horses to the railing, and ran for cover. Jennie grimaced as she pulled the soaked denim away from her legs.

"Papa!" Amber pounded on the door.

Joseph didn't answer.

"Maybe he's out looking for us. Your mom and dad would have called him."

"No," Amber insisted. "He would have met us along the way."

"In the rain?" Jennie knocked again.

Amber tried the knob. The door swung open.

Hold it, McGrady. The hairs on the back of her neck bristled. *Something is very wrong here.* "Wait." Jennie grabbed at her cousin's arm and missed.

Amber disappeared inside.

15

Jennie followed her cousin into the cabin. Lightning flashed, illuminating the storm-darkened sky. Thunder shook the ground with a crash so loud Jennie had to cover her ears.

"Jennie—" Amber screamed.

"It's okay. I'm—" Jennie gasped and pulled Amber back against her. Her gaze swept over the interior of the house. Someone had trashed it.

"Papa," Amber called. "Where are you?" She gripped Jennie's hand. "What if somebody hurt Papa too?"

"Stay here," Jennie instructed as she reached behind her to flip on the light. "I'll look in the other rooms." *Joseph could be in the house somewhere, lying wounded or . . .* Jennie wouldn't let herself complete the thought.

"I'm coming with." Rainwater dripped from Amber's hair and mingled with her tears.

"Okay. Just stay behind me and don't touch anything," Jennie said as she began picking her way across the littered floor.

In the guest bedroom, a pile of bedclothes lay in a jumbled mess. The top mattress had been shoved half off the box springs. The dresser drawers had been emptied, their contents strewn across the room. The door to Joseph's bedroom was partially closed. Jennie bit her lower lip as she tapped the door open with her foot.

It too had been ransacked. The lovely wedding quilt lay rumpled on the floor next to White Cloud's Bible and a number of other books.

"Papa's going to be so sad." Amber sighed and knelt beside the Bible. "How could anybody be so mean?"

"I don't know. They were probably looking for something." But what? Papers, a deed, a will? Apparently something small enough to fit between the pages of a book. Jennie stooped to pick up the Bible and tried to straighten and replace the fragile pages.

You shouldn't be tampering with the evidence, a part of her reminded. True, but somehow it didn't seem right to leave the hundred-year-old Bible on the floor. Jennie placed it on the nightstand.

"What's this?" Jennie reached for a triangle that peeked out from under the dresser. She withdrew a piece of crisp paper, yellowed with age. The paper's ragged edge suggested it had been ripped out of a book. A date written at the top read May 7, 1903. "It looks like a page from a diary."

Amber nodded. "The women kept a record of all the things that happened. We read them together sometimes."

"So this would be Nadi's." Jennie scanned the neatly written cursive.

Today we will surely die. White Cloud prepares to battle for the right to keep our land safe from enemy hands. Even our friend Frank Elliot and the Reverend Joshua Bennett stand against us. "You are hungry," they say—"times are hard. Sell the land and you will have more than enough to feed your family." What do they know of hard times? Why do they not understand that the Indian way is not to ravage the land, but to nurture it? The land is rich and fertile. Is it not enough to have food from the field and meat from the animals The Great Spirit sends our way? We have no need . . .

Jennie turned the page over.

. . . of earthly treasures. Perhaps it is wrong to resist, but we have

seen what the white man has done with his wealth. They have turned forests and streams into a vast wasteland in order to fill their pockets with gold and drink their whiskey. The message ended in a prayer that God would keep them safe and turn their adversaries away. Jennie wanted to read more.

"Where is the diary?" Jennie asked, glancing around the room. They found it lying in the folds of the quilt, but when Jennie turned to the place where the page had been torn out, at least two of the previous pages were missing.

Jennie replaced the torn page and set the diary beside the Bible. What treasures had Nadi written about? And more important, why would anyone destroy Joseph's house to steal them?

Jennie set the questions aside to deal with later. Right now she had to check the rest of the house.

She stepped around the debris and headed for Joseph's bathroom. The medicine cabinet door hung open, a can of shaving cream lay in the sink—a shaver beside it. The shower curtain had been ripped off several of its hooks. Jennie noticed a rust-colored smear on the white linoleum. Blood?

The sky lit up as the lightning streaked and flickered outside the bathroom window. Thunder rumbled overhead and crashed so hard it shook the house. The lights flickered and went out.

"Jennie, I'm scared."

"Me too. Come on. We'd better call your folks and have them send the sheriff out here."

With Amber still attached to her casted arm, Jennie hurried back to the kitchen. The phone line was dead. Had the wires been cut? Jennie flipped the light switch on and off. Nothing. "Looks like the storm knocked out the electricity."

"Wait. Papa's cellular phone—the one he keeps in the Ranger . . ."

Jennie raced out to the Ranger and yanked open the door. The phone was gone. She hurried back inside and locked the door. "Sorry, looks like your grandfather took it with him." Or it had been stolen. "We'll wait until the rain lets up, then ride back to the ranch."

Jennie started a fire in the fireplace, then rummaged through Joseph's closets for something dry and warm. "These will be huge on you," Jennie said, holding up a shirt and a pair of jeans, "but if we roll up the sleeves and pantlegs, and use some of that cord I saw in the kitchen, we can make them fit."

Jennie helped Amber into the oversized clothing, then went into the bathroom to strip off her soggy T-shirt and pants. She wanted a shower, but that would have to wait without power and water. Jennie settled for a quick wash. The cast smelled like two-day-old road kill and felt damp and heavy. Rain had soaked the padding and left a mushy mess. It would definitely have to be replaced. She just hoped her arm wouldn't rot off in the meantime. They'd never make the cover of *Vogue*, but at least they'd quit shivering.

When Jennie returned to the kitchen, Amber was standing near the open door intently examining something black and round. "Look at this, Jennie. Do you know what it is?"

Jennie took the object. "Looks like a camera lens," she said, turning it around. "I know of only one person around here who'd have a lens like this," Jennie said, thinking aloud. "Eric Summers. But what would his equipment be doing out here?"

Amber shrugged. "Maybe he came to take pictures of Papa."

Or maybe he came to take something else. Maggie had hired him to help develop a new brochure. According to Heather, Joseph knew about Eric. Maybe Heather had brought him here. Still, it seemed strange that Eric would lose something as important as a camera lens. Jennie thought about the blood smear in the bathroom.

"What are you thinking about, Jennie?" Amber pulled at her arm.

"Just wondering about this lens."

"Maybe Eric dropped it when he got shot."

"Maybe." Jennie didn't want to think about that possibility. "Heather and Eric could have come here to say goodbye." Jennie took a deep breath, not knowing how much of what she was thinking she could reveal to Amber.

Whoever had shot Eric, and sent him home on Heather's horse, could have abducted Heather *and* Joseph. She debated whether to leave the lens at the house or bring it with her. She knew better than to disturb a crime scene, but Amber had already picked it up. She opted to bring the lens along and give it to Jeff.

When the rain let up, Jennie and Amber checked the stables but found no sign of Joseph. They did, however, find an Appaloosa wandering free. "It's Hazen's," Amber insisted.

"This couldn't be Hazen's," Jennie argued. "He took off this morning, when he . . ." Her argument died when she realized Thunder's halter was still on. Had they gotten Hazen too? Had Danielson's army moved in? Were he and Chad Elliot working together? Were she and Amber next?

No, McGrady, don't even think it. Concentrate on getting Amber out of here.

Before they left, Jennie fixed them each a sandwich and packed a few snacks and some emergency equipment—a first-aid kit, flashlight, matches, and rain gear—in saddlebags she borrowed from the barn. By two-thirty they were on their way back to the dude ranch.

Even with the sun leaking through scattered holes in the bullet gray sky, Jennie worried about getting back safely since they were returning a different way. Amber had insisted they take the higher trail for fear the one they'd come in on would be flooded.

The sunshine lasted all of ten minutes. The holes in the

sky closed up, heavy clouds rolled in and opened fire on them again with a mixture of hail and rain. The girls donned the rain capes they'd packed and rode on.

Fifteen minutes later Amber pulled Cinnamon up next to a creek. "The water's up, but we can still make it across."

Jennie could barely hear her over the water's roar. "Maybe we'd better go back."

"No, we can make it."

Jennie wasn't so sure. The stream was a floodwater brown—so churned up with mud, it was hard to tell its depth.

"Come on." Amber spurred Cinnamon forward, but the horse pulled back in protest. Finally at Amber's insistence the horse plunged into the water.

"Amber," Jennie warned, "this is not a good idea. Let's go back." Gabby, apparently not wanting to be left behind, shuddered, then moved ahead, as though forging swollen streams was too great an adventure to miss.

They had nearly reached the other side when Cinnamon stumbled and fell. "Jennie, help." Amber toppled off Cinnamon's back as her horse tried to right herself. Jennie grabbed for the child. The rain slick poncho slipped from her grasp. She watched in horror as Amber's red-gold curls disappeared into the murky, swirling water.

16

"Amber!" Jennie struggled to keep her own balance. Gabby slipped on the eroded bank, but managed to regain his footing to escape the swollen creek. Jennie sprang from the saddle and raced downstream to where Amber floated to the surface, sputtering and kicking, then Jennie plunged into the icy waters in another attempt to rescue her.

Despite the awkwardness of the heavy, water-soaked cast, Jennie managed to grab Amber and drag her out of the water. "Stop kicking," she yelled when Amber's boots connected with her shins. "I've got you."

Amber kept thrashing.

Jennie guessed the water to be about four feet deep where she was standing, but fighting the current and her cousin was like battling a tidal wave. It took all her strength to plant her feet against the rocks and propel them toward shore.

She pushed Amber onto the bank, then climbed out and pulled the now limp child to safety. After making sure Amber was okay, Jennie collapsed on the wet ground. She hauled in as much of the moist air as her heaving lungs could hold. A stream of muddy brown water trickled out of her cast.

A few minutes later, Amber crawled closer and lay her head on Jennie's chest. "Guess we shouldn't have tried to go across."

"Guess not." Jennie closed her eyes as the rain pelted her

face. She soothed Amber's saturated curls. "But we made it." She sighed and rose onto her elbows when Amber sat up. "We'd better get home."

"My leg hurts." Amber leaned forward and lifted the plastic cape. Her jeans were torn at the knee and rain-diluted blood streamed from an inch-long gash. Amber stared at the wound for several seconds, then let out a wail Jennie felt certain could be heard in the next county. Her little tomboy cousin wasn't quite so tough after all.

"Shh. It's okay, Amber. Take it easy. I've got a first-aid kit in one of the saddlebags." Jennie glanced around expecting to see Gabby and Cinnamon nearby. They were close all right—only about fifty feet away, but they may as well have been in Albuquerque. The horses were grazing contentedly on the other side of the swollen creek.

"What in the. . . ?" Jennie stifled a cry of alarm. With surprising calm, she said, "First of all, Amber, I need to stop the bleeding."

"No! Don't touch it." Amber flapped her legs up and down.

"It won't hurt, I promise. Just hold still." Jennie peeled off her wet neckerchief, wrung it out, tied it around Amber's knee, and kept a steady pressure for several minutes while she tried to assess their situation.

Jennie soon realized she'd gotten turned around while trying to rescue Amber. Dancing Waters still lay on the other side of the creek.

Amber's sobs turned to whimpers. "What are we gonna do about the horses? How are we going to get home?"

Jennie had no idea. She wasn't about to wade through the creek again, but they couldn't stay where they were either. If the rain didn't let up, the entire valley would soon be under water.

"Come on." Jennie stood and extended a hand to Amber. "Let's get out of here. We'll walk back to Joseph's cabin. We may not have electricity, but we can build a fire and get some dry clothes."

Amber got halfway up, then sank back to the ground. "Ow! I can't walk."

"I know it hurts, but you have to try. Here." Jennie removed their slick rain ponchos, then knelt down in front of her. "Put your arm around my neck. I'll give you a piggyback ride." Jennie hoisted Amber onto her back, then settled the plastic over both of them like a tent. She crossed the mushy ground and headed for the highest point. After a few yards Jennie began altering her plans.

"Where are we going, Jennie?" Amber tightened her hold. "This isn't the way to Papa's."

"I know. But I can't carry you that far." Jennie stopped to adjust her heavy load. "I'm hoping there's some kind of cave or overhang up there." She pointed to an odd-looking rock formation. "Maybe we can stay there until the storm passes—or until help comes."

"No. Wait. Let's go to Papa's secret place. It's closer."

Jennie sighed. "This isn't a game, Amber."

"I know. But this is a for-real cave and it's up there—behind those bushes. Come on. I'll show you."

Jennie walked in the direction Amber pointed. When Amber told her to stop, Jennie set her cousin down on a boulder, then lifted her own rain-soaked bangs from her forehead. "I don't see a cave. Are you sure this is the right spot?"

"You can't see it from here. That's why it's secret. You have to go behind those bushes. There's a rock—only it isn't a rock, it's a door. You push this lever and the rock moves. Papa says it's so no one would find the gold."

"A rock that's a door? Gold? Come on, Amber, be serious."

"I am." Amber scooted closer. "There's a lever in the rocks behind these bushes."

Jennie moved the thick brush aside. Sure enough, a metal

handle protruded from a crevice. Following Amber's instructions she pulled it to one side.

The mountain itself seemed to groan and squeak as the rock that was really a door shuddered, then moved along a narrow track. When it stopped, it left a gaping black hole. "I can't believe it." Amber had been right. Except for one thing. This was no cave. It was a mine. But why. . . ?

"See, I told you. Only you gotta promise not to tell anyone. Papa said if the wrong people found out, they would destroy the mountain." Amber set a rock under the lever and Jennie helped her inside.

"What's the rock for?" Jennie asked.

"To make sure the door stays open. Yuk." Amber covered her face with her arm to ward off the spider webs that had been woven across the opening.

Jennie waved her hand back and forth to clear the webs away, hoping she wouldn't encounter the spiders themselves. The mine smelled musty and metallic, like an old dirt cellar. Except for the mottled patches of daylight coming through the branches, the mine shaft was dark as tar.

Jennie didn't want to leave her cousin or the safety of the mine, but she needed to get back down to the creek and figure out a way to get to the horses. Without the horses they could be stuck in the wilderness until help came or until Amber could walk. That could be days. Besides that, the first-aid equipment and supplies were still in the saddlebags. Maybe they'd survive without the food and supplies she'd packed, but Jennie didn't want to take the chance.

She settled Amber inside the opening and out of the rain.

"Listen," Jennie said, uncertain how to begin. "I have to go back down—see if I can get to the horses. I don't want to leave you, but I have to. I'll come back as soon as I can. Will you be okay?"

"I—I think so. Just hurry."

Jennie scrambled over the rocks and soon raced along the

sodden ground. Gabby and Cinnamon still waited in the meadow, only now the creek had risen. It raged with even more fury than it had before. Jennie scanned the banks looking for a fallen log, a tree, anything that might help her get across. Nothing.

She followed the creek downstream, praying with each step for a miracle. Her mind was so intent on her thoughts that she almost missed it. About half a mile from the place they'd tried to cross before, the creek widened, then separated, leaving a four-foot wide island in the middle. Two streams to cross, but the creek's energy would be divided. At least she hoped that would be the case.

Jennie took a deep breath, then tested the water. One foot in. Water swirled around her ankle. Next step, the same. With the next she sank to her knees and nearly lost her footing. She waded several more feet to the island, heaving a sigh of relief as her foot connected with the rocks. Crossing the island, she tilted her face to the sky. "Amber needs me, God," Jennie whispered. "And I need those horses. Please help me get across."

Jennie forded the second part of the creek more easily than the first and ran back upstream to where the horses still waited. God must have heard her pleas. Even the rain had let up a little.

Since the horses could easily cross at the spot she had, Jennie grabbed both horses' reins. On unsteady legs, Jennie climbed onto the saddle and headed back downstream. A few minutes later, they stood on the island, ready to make the final leg of what had seemed an impossible journey.

Jennie took a deep breath and urged Gabby forward. At that moment a white-hot streak of lightning slammed into a nearby tree. Both horses panicked. "Oh no," she moaned, "not again." Heaven rumbled with a steady roll of thunder as it crescendoed, then crashed. The entire mountainside seemed to explode as the tree splintered and crashed to the ground.

Jennie held tight to the saddlehorn and waved her casted arm wildly to keep from falling. Her hands had grown stiff and numb from the cold. Too late, Jennie remembered she held both of the horses' reins. Cinnamon rose on her back legs and pawed at the air, yanking Jennie sideways. Jennie released the mare's reins, but not soon enough. As if in slow motion, gravity propelled her downward.

Jennie landed on her hip and shoulders on the rocky ground and rolled to the side to escape the horses' hooves. Gabby reared, throwing the saddlebags off his back and onto the ground. The terrified horses bolted and ran. Jennie rolled over on her stomach and cried.

It wasn't in her nature to give up, but then nature had never tried to beat her to death until now. She ignored the insistent voice in her head that told her to get up and keep going. She hurt too much to move.

She rested her head on her uncasted arm and cried. After a few minutes she tried giving herself a pep talk. *Come on, McGrady. Get up. Okay, so you lost the horses. At least you've got the saddlebags.* Still, she didn't move.

Rain dripped steadily on her back and mingled with her tears. Rocks dug into her stomach and thighs. Bone-chilling water seeped into her already wet clothing and inside her cast. But that didn't make sense. She'd fallen onto dry land.

Jennie raised her head. The raging creek had covered the tiny island. The saddlebags were already floating away and if she didn't get out of there fast she'd be the next to go.

17

"Come back here!" Jennie scrambled to her feet.

The current lifted and dragged the heavy saddlebags over the rocks. "After all I went through to get you, you're not going to just float away." Jennie lunged for them. Despite the pain that now wracked her body, she settled them over her left shoulder then stumbled across the ever widening creek.

"Come on, McGrady, just one more step—a little farther." Jennie muttered the words over again as she slogged through the ankle-deep water in the meadow, then crawled up the slippery hillside to where she had left Amber. She collapsed near the mine's entrance, shivering, exhausted, and near tears.

"Oh please, no more." In the last few hours she'd been through more adventures than Harrison Ford in *Raiders of the Lost Ark* and apparently the show wasn't over. Jennie stared at the shrubs covering the opening to the mine shaft. Someone had closed the entrance.

Don't panic, she told herself. *Maybe Amber closed it herself.* Jennie doubted that. No ten-year-old child would deliberately lock herself in a dark mine shaft.

Steeling herself against what she might find, Jennie pulled the lever. As before, the metal door moved across the track. She took the flashlight out of the damp saddlebags, switched it on, and stepped inside. "Amber?" She called tentatively at first, then increased the volume when no one answered. "Amber, are you in here?"

Jennie crept deeper into the darkness that hovered beyond the reaches of her small light, listening, waiting for a response. None came. She took another step and collided with another curtain of spider webs. She stifled a scream and brushed the dusty webs away. "Amber," Jennie called again.

Still no answer. Jennie wondered how far back the cave went and if there was another opening. And what besides spiders lived in there. *Bats, probably, and snakes . . .*

"Stop it, McGrady," she reprimanded herself. "You are not going to scare yourself. Amber's gone and in two seconds you'll be out of here." But then what? As if answering her question, the door clicked, then rumbled closed, devouring the last traces of light from the opening.

"No!" Jennie dropped the flashlight and raced toward the door. She clawed at the wet, slippery surface, willing it to stop. Her efforts had about as much effect as a mouse trying to stop a train. She pulled her fingers back as the door snapped shut.

Panic stalked her like a rattlesnake, and struck. Its venom seeped into her pores. Jennie leaned back against the door. Her knees collapsed beneath her.

Now she understood why Amber had positioned a rock under the lever to keep the door open. She should have paid more attention. She closed her eyes and wrapped her arms around herself to stop the shivering. The terror she'd felt a moment before began to drain away, leaving her numb and cold.

Jennie wondered how low her body temperature had dropped and how long she would last. She was well aware of the dangers of hypothermia. "Oh, God," she whimpered, "what am I going to do?"

Only the silence answered. Yet in the stillness Jennie began to feel a strange sense of peace. She took several deep breaths and, after a few moments, opened her eyes, more curious now than afraid. Jennie leaned forward and rescued the flashlight she'd dropped and directed the beam over the mine walls and the wood supports that framed it. She forced her brain to focus on the possibility of escape rather than on her cold, wet clothing, or the numbness in her hands and fingers.

Think, McGrady. There has to be a way out. Just stay calm and think. If Joseph had devised a mechanism for opening the door on the outside, wouldn't he also place one inside?

Not necessarily. It could have been designed as a trap. There may be bones of men or women who found the cave, but who had taken the secret with them to their graves. Jennie tried to still her imagination before it zoomed out of control, but it had already boarded a fast train. She thought of the darkness and wondered how far back the mine shaft went and how many old bones it held in its depths.

"I told you to stop it, McGrady." Jennie tried to ignore the frightening images screaming through her head and focused on the dirt walls and wooden supports. Two wires ran along the right side of the door, but Jennie found no lever that might trigger the mechanism from the inside.

Was this the end? Trapped in a cave—a tomb. The revelation didn't frighten her like it should have. Maybe the encroaching hypothermia had numbed her brain cells. Or maybe, knowing in her heart that her spirit would live forever, she wasn't that afraid of dying.

"Poor Joseph," Jennie said aloud. He'd be heartbroken to know a tool he devised to keep people from discovering his secret mine had been her demise and maybe Amber's.

Amber. Was she still in the cave? Perhaps she'd fallen asleep. Or maybe she'd been injured more seriously than Jennie had first thought. She illuminated the mine floor as far as the flashlight beam reached, then reluctantly stood and went in deeper. Jennie called again. Still no answer.

After the first few steps, Jennie paused to examine the

glimmering substance on the walls. She brushed her fingers over a large section of iridescent rock. The flashlight's meager beam didn't allow her to see much, but it did reflect off the walls enough for Jennie to see the sparkling veins of—what? Jennie picked up a chunk of the shiny metal from the ground. Gold? Silver? Silver had been mined in this area for over a hundred years. But this looked like gold—probably iron pyrite or what miners called fool's gold. It had to be, she rationalized. That much real gold would have been mined years ago.

Or would it? What had Nadi said in her diary? *The Indian way is not to ravage the land, but to nurture it. . . . We have no need of earthly treasures . . . we have seen what the white man has done with his wealth. They have turned forests and streams into a vast wasteland . . .*

Jennie gasped. "White Cloud was preparing to fight for their land." *The mine? Oh wow! If that's true, this could be real gold.* "And worth millions," she murmured aloud. "A definite motive for murder." Possibilities flooded her head. Did Danielson know about the mine? Chad Elliot probably did. Who else?

Jennie slipped the rock in her pocket and yawned. Despite the excitement of possibly finding gold, she was growing weary. Probably as a result of the cold. Or maybe she was just plain exhausted. Jennie lowered herself to the ground and wrapped the plastic poncho more tightly around her. Maybe her body would generate enough heat to warm her limbs and send her temperature back up to normal. She leaned back against the dirt wall, wrapped her arms around her knees, and rested her head on them.

Why? The question hung in her fading consciousness. Joseph had a mine that could be worth millions. Why was it mined in the first place? If Joseph and his father didn't believe in tearing up the land, why build the mine shaft?

"Maybe he didn't," Jennie answered her own question.

"Maybe Frank Elliot or his son did." In reading the history of the Nez Perce Indians, Jennie remembered how the settlers had gone onto the reservation and found gold. Since the Indians believed that one could not own the land, white miners often went into areas designated as Indian territory and if they found gold, claimed the land for themselves. As far as she knew, Dancing Waters had never been part of a reservation, but suppose Elliot had ignored White Cloud's ownership, found gold, then tried to mine it against White Cloud's wishes? According to Joseph, though, Frank Elliot was a good man who made certain White Cloud was cared for.

Greed has corrupted a lot of people, Jennie reasoned. *Besides, his son, William, might have known about the mine. He'd been desperate for money. But if he were sitting on a gold mine, why sell off all the property?*

Other questions surfaced. Where did Eric fit into it all? And Danielson? Did she care? Did she want to spend her last moments trying to solve a mystery? Yes, but what good would it do? She didn't have enough information. She needed to take in a sample of the gold to have it analyzed. And she'd have to go to the library or courthouse to check on land use. "If . . . when I get out of here—"

The flashlight tumbled out of her numb fingers and clunked as it hit the ground. She thought about retrieving it, but couldn't make her body move. Her thoughts drifted to another tomb, owned by another Joseph. Jesus had been buried there after His death on the cross. Three days later the stone had been rolled away, and an angel told His followers the good news. *"He is risen."*

Three days. Would someone come to the mine and discover her lifeless body? Or would she somehow be resurrected? Jennie didn't feel like thinking anymore—didn't want to move. It was as if her entire body was shutting down. Was this what it felt like to die? The question went unanswered as Jennie closed her eyes.

18

Jennie smelled fire.

Its dry heat permeated and relaxed her cold, tense muscles. It crackled and sizzled, consuming wood laced with pitch.

And she smelled frybread.

"Hmm," she moaned softly, wanting to open her eyes but afraid that her warm, wonderful dream would vanish, leaving her alone in the cold, dark mine.

"She's waking up, Papa." The voice so reminded Jennie of Nick, tears gathered behind her eyelids. Would she ever see her little brother again? Or Mom? Her tears escaped their boundaries and slid over her temples and into her hair.

"Oh, Papa, she's crying."

"Hush, Tiponi. You will wake her."

"But she's sad. Maybe she's hurt."

Jennie pressed her hands to her eyes, squeezing out the moisture. Her eyes drifted open. Amber smiled and leaned over her, their noses nearly touching.

"I told Papa you were awake but he didn't believe me." Her eyes clouded in concern. "You're okay, aren't you, Jennie? I told Papa to wait longer. We looked for you. He thought you went back to the ranch and . . ."

"Whoa. Slow down. What are you talking about?" Jennie was beginning to adjust to the possibility that she'd been rescued and that this wasn't a dream after all. Joseph brought in a tray, set it on the coffee table, and helped her sit up. She was in Joseph's cabin, lying on the supple leather couch. Her wet clothes had been exchanged for her own clean dry ones—the jeans and chambray shirt she'd left at the cabin earlier. It was dark outside, but inside, a dozen or so candles bathed the room in subdued light. "How did I get here?"

"I will answer your questions in a moment." Joseph propped pillows behind her. "First, you must eat." He placed a tray on her lap. A piece of frybread, buttered and sprinkled with cinnamon and sugar, lay on a plate next to a bowl of what Joseph called venison stew.

"Thank you," Jennie murmured as she lifted the warm frybread to her mouth. It tasted so good, Jennie didn't care where she was for the moment, or how she'd gotten there.

Amber sat cross-legged on the rug near Jennie's head and watched her. Joseph poked at the glowing chunks of wood in the fireplace.

"What happened to you out there, Amber?" Jennie asked after taking another spoonful of Joseph's stew.

"Papa found me."

Jennie frowned. "How did you know where she was?"

Amber answered. "He knew we had been here at his cabin and came after us. We didn't want to leave you, but we looked everywhere for you. Papa thought you went back to the ranch. Where were you?"

"After I left you at the mine, I went downstream to find a shallow spot where I could get across safely—you remember. I wanted to get the horses and the first-aid kit." Jennie explained her misadventures in retrieving the horses, losing them again, nearly drowning, and being locked in the mine. She shifted her gaze from Amber to Joseph. "How did you know to come back for me?"

"When we got back here, Daddy called on the cellular and told us that Gabby and Cinnamon had come back without you. They sent out a search party. I told Papa we should go back and check the mine."

"That she did. I knew you'd try to get back to Amber if you could."

"That door you rigged at the mine locked me in. You should put a release mechanism inside."

"There is one, but it is hidden behind a beam. I'm sorry you could not find it."

Jennie finished off the soup and frybread, then asked, "Are you sure this is for real and that I'm not still dreaming? I mean, how could I not remember coming here?"

"You were exhausted." Joseph took her tray.

Jennie snuggled back into the cushions. She was still tired. "What time is it?"

"Ten-thirty. You should rest now. The rain has finally stopped. Perhaps the waters will recede enough for us to get you and Amber back to Dancing Waters. You need to have that cast replaced." He set the tray down on the counter, then returned to the living room. "And you, Tiponi. Off to bed now. It's way past your bedtime, and we'll both be in trouble if your mother finds out I let you stay up so long."

Amber started to argue but must have caught the stern look in Joseph's eyes. "Okay, but can Jennie sleep with me?"

"If she wants." He glanced at Jennie.

"I might be in later." Although she didn't say so, Jennie needed to talk with Joseph privately.

Amber gave Jennie a good-night kiss and headed for the bathroom. "Will you tell me some stories, Papa?"

"Not tonight. It is much too late."

"Joseph?" Jennie didn't know where to start. "There's so much I need to talk to you about. Your house, the mine, and . . ." Jennie glanced around, realizing the mess had been cleaned up. "Did you call the sheriff about the break-in? I tried to when I was here this morning, but the phone was dead. We were so worried about you."

Joseph's lips parted in a half smile as he nodded. "It still is. And the power. I'm sorry you have carried this burden. I went hunting this morning. When I returned and saw that someone had broken in, I called the sheriff on my cellular phone. Like me, he suspects it was vandalism. As far as I can tell, there is nothing missing."

"The diary—there are some pages missing." Jennie told him about the connection she'd made with Nadi's entry and the mine. "Do you think whoever broke in was looking for information about the mine?"

Joseph's brows knitted in a frown. "It's possible. Though I—"

"Papa. I'm ready."

"I must say good-night to my granddaughter, then we will talk." While he tucked Amber in, Jennie tossed the blanket aside, used the bathroom, then padded to the kitchen to fix Joseph and herself some herb tea.

Having retrieved Nadi's diary, Joseph returned to the living room and sank wearily into the chair closest to Jennie. He opened the book to where Jennie had inserted the loose page.

Joseph read for a moment, then leaned back and closed his eyes. "You may be right. Nadi writes of the mine just before this page. It doesn't give the location—only the legend of how it came to be. Whoever broke in may have been searching for a map. In which case he would have been disappointed."

"You don't have a map?"

"To my knowledge there never was one."

"Tell me the legend about the mine. Is there gold in it?"

"It's late."

"Oh please. I'll never be able to sleep until I know. Besides, you need to drink your tea."

Joseph sighed and picked up his cup. "Yes, it is gold." He reached into his shirt pocket, then tucked something into her hand. It was the rock she'd picked up on the mine floor.

"There is no need to have it analyzed."

Jennie flushed. "How did you know I was going to?"

"I am beginning to know you."

"I'm sorry for taking it." He held up his hand when she tried to return it.

"You may keep this as a souvenir of your visit. I think it best, however, if you don't tell anyone where it came from just yet."

"I won't say anything. But you still haven't told me why all the secrecy. And if you didn't want the gold to be mined, why is there a mine shaft?" Jennie took a tentative sip of the hot tea.

"As I mentioned before, Frank Elliot deeded 500 acres of Dancing Waters land over to White Cloud—my father—in 1889. What neither of them knew was that an old Dutch miner named Henry VonHassen had found gold here in 1885."

"How could they not know?"

"Over the years, VonHassen developed quite a reputation in Cottonwood. He'd come into town every couple of months with a pouchful of the purest gold the assayers had ever seen. The old man kept pretty much to himself. Never staked a claim or told anyone where he'd been mining. He led everyone to believe he'd just picked up pebbles here and there in the mountain streams. And for good reason—the property wasn't his." Joseph rocked back and forth as if waiting for the rest of story to come to him.

"Did anyone ever follow him and see where the gold came from?"

"Many tried. VonHassen figured on folks doing just that. He'd lead them into the mountains, get them good and lost, then come back to the mine."

"And neither White Cloud nor Elliot knew?"

Joseph stilled the rocker and took another sip of tea. "Not until White Cloud found him in a ravine the winter of 1897.

He'd fallen from a cliff. White Cloud tried to save him." Joseph frowned. "The old miner only lasted a couple days, but he told my father about the mine. I suppose he wanted to make amends before he died."

"In the diary, Nadi said Frank Elliot and a Reverend Bennett were trying to get White Cloud to work the mine. How did they know about it?" Jennie leaned forward to place her cup on the table, then tucked her legs under her.

"White Cloud told Frank about the mine and offered to give him back the land. He refused it and promised to keep the mine a secret."

"So the Reverend leaked the information?" Jennie asked.

Joseph shook his head. "No, he was not the kind of man who betrayed a trust."

"Then how?"

"VonHassen was found on White Cloud's land and people assumed his mine was there. Folks started telling stories and pretty soon treasure hunters were swarming all over those hills looking for the old Dutchman's mine."

"But they never found it," Jennie added.

"VonHassen had hidden it well. Eventually, the excitement died down and people lost interest."

"Until now. Do you think the mine is behind all that's happened at Dancing Waters—I mean the explosion and Heather?" Jennie bolted upright. "Oh, Heather . . . and Eric. Did you know about Eric getting shot and Heather being kidnapped? I can't believe I'm just now telling you."

Joseph placed his hands on his knees for leverage, then stood. "You have had much to occupy your mind today. But, yes, my son told me what happened. You must rest now. We'll talk more in the morning."

Jennie ignored his attempt to leave and kept talking. "Have they found her?"

"No."

"What about the ranch? Did you know Jeff was making

plans to meet the kidnapper's demands and deed the ranch over to Chad Elliot? That's what Amber was so upset about."

"I have spoken to my son." Joseph stoked the fire and added another log. "We will do what must be done to obtain Heather's release."

"But . . ."

"Good night, Jennie."

"I found something else," Jennie persisted, not wanting to give up until she'd gotten more of her questions answered. "A camera lens. I thought it might belong to Eric and wondered if Heather had brought him here."

Joseph shook his head. "Where is the lens?"

"In the saddlebags. If it is Eric's, he must have dropped it when he was searching the house." Jennie frowned. "But how could he have known about the mine? Unless . . . Did Heather know?"

"It did not seem wise to share the secret with the twins. They are not yet ready."

"Do you think Chad Elliot knows about the mine and maybe that's why he's so adamant about getting Dancing Waters back?"

"It is possible. He may have found a reference to the mine among his father's belongings." Joseph blew out all the candles but one, which he handed to Jennie. "There's a toothbrush and towels in the bathroom. If you need anything else, let me know."

"Um . . . could I ask you one more question?"

Joseph hesitated. "And what might that be?"

"Uncle Jeff told me what you said about letting me investigate. I just wanted to thank you and ask why—I mean, most adults would just tell me to mind my own business."

"Your grandmother calls you an eagle. Do you know about eagles, Jennie?"

"Only that they're birds of prey. And I love to watch them fly."

"To capture an eagle is like roping the wind. They are not easily caught. When an eagle is trapped, it will literally beat itself to death trying to escape. It is in your nature to seek answers, just as it is in the eagle's nature to soar in the heavens."

"I'm not getting anywhere with this case. I don't know if I can do it. I don't want to disappoint you and Uncle Jeff."

"Do you know more than you did this morning?" Joseph asked.

"Yes, but—"

"That is good." His smile affirmed her even more than his words. "Good night, Brave Eagle. Sleep well. Tonight we will pray for wisdom and tomorrow we will seek truth."

Jennie washed by candlelight, ignoring the bedraggled-looking creature that stared back at her in the mirror. *Sheesh, McGrady. You look more like Ruffled Feather than Brave Eagle.* She quickly tugged the rats out of her hair and brushed her teeth, then slipped into the flannel nightshirt Joseph had set out for her.

She eased her aching body under the covers and blew out the candle. Outside the living room window the subdued light from the porch created an odd mixture of shadows.

One of those shadows took on human form and began to move. Or had it? The hair on the back of her neck stood on end. *For Pete's sake, McGrady. It's probably just the wind. Besides, you're safe here.* Only, Jennie didn't feel safe. She threw the covers aside. She wouldn't rest until she'd confronted her fear and taken a look outside.

A figure moved out of the shadows and crept to the window.

Jennie stifled a scream as she looked point-blank into the intruder's face.

19

The figure straightened and stepped toward the front porch. Though she hadn't clearly seen his face, she recognized him.

Jennie willed her heart and stomach back to their respective places. She let Hazen in and locked the door behind him.

"What are you doing here?" Jennie asked, keeping her voice low. "More to the point, why did you take off like that this morning?"

He limped over to the couch and dropped onto it, moaning as he made contact.

"Hazen?"

He pulled up his legs and held his stomach. "It's nothing. Just get me an ice bag, will you?"

Jennie fumbled for the matches and lit the candle. She gasped when she saw his face. Dried blood made a path from his nostril to his chin. His lower lip was swollen and split. "What happened?" Jennie asked as she hurried to the freezer. "Who did this to you?"

She found a package of blue ice in the freezer and wrapped it in a towel, then grabbed a clean washcloth and wet it. When she reached his side, she handed the ice pack to him. "I'm not sure where you want it."

"Me either." He placed it over his swollen lip and bruised left cheek.

"So, what happened?" She gingerly dabbed at the dried blood.

Hazen peered at her through the eye that wasn't swollen shut. "Why don't you ask your friend Marty?"

"Marty did this? I thought . . ."

"Just forget it, will you?" He batted her hand away. "It's not your concern."

"Hazen!" Joseph's voice was harsh yet at the same time held a touch of compassion.

Jennie jumped. As usual, she hadn't heard him come in.

Hazen swung his legs off the couch and grimaced. "Geez, Gramps, do you have to sneak up on people that way?"

Instead of answering, Joseph ordered him to lie back down so he could examine his wounds. After a few moments he straightened. "I see nothing broken, but I want you to see a doctor tomorrow."

"I don't need a doctor." Hazen winced when he tried to sit up again.

Joseph sat in his rocker and motioned for Jennie to sit as well. "Now, we shall hear how my grandson spent his day."

For what seemed an eternity, Hazen looked up at the moose head on the wall, then at Jennie, and finally at his grandfather. "I wanted to find Heather. Figured Danielson had her. Marty's been pretty steamed since she dumped him."

"So you went to confront Marty and he beat you up?" Jennie asked.

"Not exactly. I rode over to Danielson's and told Marty he'd better let my sister go or I'd bash his head in. He told me he didn't know where Heather was and said I should ask Eric," Hazen huffed. "Like he didn't know Eric had been shot. My guess is that Marty's the one who shot him. Anyway, he started to leave and I nailed him."

Joseph shook his head in apparent disapproval.

147

"And he nailed you back?" Jennie prodded, wishing he'd get to the point.

"No. I took off. Thought I'd go up to the Danielsons' hunting cabin and check that out in case he'd hidden her up there. Never got that far. I stopped here to get a g—" he glanced nervously at Joseph. "A gun. A couple of militia guys caught up with me out in the woods behind the barn and . . ." Hazen raised his arm and covered his eyes.

"Did you recognize them?" Jennie asked.

"Yeah. They work for Danielson."

"Are you sure Marty sent them?" Jennie asked.

"Either him or his dad. They kept swearing at me and calling me names. Said if I was going to act like a half-breed savage they'd treat me like one."

Jennie looked at Joseph. The break-in. She hadn't said it aloud but he responded as though she had. His nod encouraged her to pursue her thoughts. "Hazen, do you know what time you got here?"

"No. Probably about an hour after I left home, I guess." He lowered his arm and looked at her. "Why?"

Jennie told him about the break-in and asked if the men who beat him up had also ransacked the cabin.

"I don't know. Could be, I guess. All I know is I woke up long enough to crawl into the barn to get out of the rain. Been there ever since."

"That explains why your horse was here. You must have been out there when Amber and I came. We looked around, but didn't see anyone. I feel awful that you were out there all that time."

"You couldn't have known." Joseph sighed. "Jennie, perhaps you could heat up a bowl of stew for Hazen while I help him get cleaned up."

"Sure." Glad for something to do besides stare at her handsome cousin's disfigured face, Jennie put a kettle on for tea and heated some leftover venison stew. There was no frybread left, so she made toast and set it all on a placemat at the table.

After a few minutes, Joseph and Hazen returned. Hazen still looked like he'd been used as a punching bag. He devoured the stew and asked for seconds.

After he'd eaten, Hazen returned to the couch where Jennie had been sleeping. Jennie headed for the guest room where she would share the bed with Amber. Hazen and his grandfather were still talking when Jennie left.

"Ow," Hazen moaned, "I hurt all over."

Jennie hadn't intended to listen, but their voices flowed clearly through the inch-wide opening under the door.

"It serves you right for thinking you can fight battles with fists and guns."

"How else do we fight them? Words mean nothing to men like Danielson," Hazen said. "If I don't defend our honor, who will? You and Dad and this non-violence garbage don't cut it."

Joseph sighed audibly. "You do not defend our honor by fighting—you dishonor us. Honor is given to each of us by our Creator. No man or woman can strip it away—you can only do that to yourself. You, my son, dishonor yourself by being ashamed of your heritage."

"Spare me the lecture. Marty and his dad have Heather and I'll prove it. Tomorrow I'm riding up to their hunting lodge."

"Even if they are guilty, they would not be foolish enough to keep her there."

"I'm still going. You coming along?"

"No. I must take Amber and Jennie back to Dancing Waters. And I would like to have a word with the sheriff. Perhaps he has learned more about Heather and Eric."

"Why bother? We both know Jake and Marty did it. Danielson makes no secret of the fact that he wants your land for his military training."

"We may not believe in what Danielson does, my son, but he does not strike me as the kind of man who would kidnap a young girl."

"Why not? It's not like the sheriff is going to arrest him. Sheriff Mason is one of them."

"Enough. We will speak no more of this tonight. I'd like you to come with me tomorrow when I take the girls home. We will need to file a complaint against the men who beat you; and your father will want to see you."

A short time later, as she lay in the dark, quiet room, Jennie let Joseph's words wash over her again and again. *Honor is given by our Creator. No man can strip it away—you can only do that to yourself.* Joseph had said that Hazen dishonored himself by being ashamed of his Indian heritage. Along with her prayers for wisdom that night, Jennie prayed that Hazen would learn to honor and respect himself and that Heather would be found safe and alive.

When Jennie woke up the next morning, Hazen was gone. Joseph did not mention the fact, so Jennie didn't either. She hoped Hazen was wrong and that Marty and his father didn't have Heather hidden in their cabin. He'd be placing himself in danger again, and this time he might not be so lucky.

After breakfast, Amber and Jennie gathered their belongings and piled into Joseph's Ford Ranger. He'd reached the end of the driveway when Hazen galloped in as though he were being chased by a gang of marauders. He stopped beside the Ranger and handed Joseph a pink-and-white feathered barrette.

"It's Heather's. This proves she was there. They must have moved her yesterday after I talked to them."

"You are certain it was in the cabin?" Joseph stroked the feather, his brows knitted together.

"I found it on the floor. Don't you see? It's proof. I'm heading back home to tell Dad." He took the feather back, turned Thunder around, and raced away. "I'll meet you there," he yelled over his shoulder.

Jennie wished she could be as excited about Hazen's "proof" as he was. Unfortunately, it meant nothing. Heather could have gone to the cabin while she and Marty had been dating. Hazen could have planted it there. The worst part of it was that Hazen had tampered with the evidence. She doubted the sheriff would even believe him.

Back at the ranch, Maggie and Jeff welcomed Amber and Jennie home. Maggie promptly whisked Amber off to help her change and do all the things worried mothers do. Jennie followed Joseph and her uncle into Jeff's office.

Joseph brought his son up to date. Jennie then offered her version of the break-in, telling him about the diary's missing pages and the camera lens she'd found. She'd just finished when Hazen walked in. He tossed Heather's barrette on the desk.

Jeff listened as Hazen made vehement accusations against the Danielsons, then said, "I think it's time we pool our resources here and do a little brainstorming. I just got off the phone with Sheriff Mason, and he thinks he's got the case wrapped up. To be honest, I'm not convinced."

"You mean he actually arrested Marty and his dad?" Hazen asked.

"No. He's arrested Eric."

20

"What?" Hazen stared at his father as though he'd sided with the enemy.

"Apparently, Eric confessed to breaking into Dad's place. He also says he was the gunman Jennie and Amber saw in the llama pasture." Jeff fingered his daughter's barrette. "He hasn't confessed to Rick's murder or to kidnapping Heather, but Sam seems to think a full confession is forthcoming."

"That's crazy." Hazen exploded from his chair. "He's using Eric as a scapegoat because he can't—or won't—arrest Danielson. Eric didn't kill Rick. Rick killed himself. He—"

"Wait a minute," Jeff interrupted. "What are you saying?"

Joseph stood as if to intervene.

Hazen sank back into his chair, pale and shaking. "I—I saw him, Dad."

Joseph placed his hands on his grandson's shoulders. "Go on, son."

"I saw Rick throw something into the gas tank. He tried to run, but tripped. He meant to—to kill you." Hazen covered his eyes with his hand.

Jeff's dark eyes softened. "Why didn't you speak up before now?"

"I couldn't." He jerked his hand away from his face. "If I'd acted quicker, maybe I could have saved you. I didn't even yell at you to get out of the way."

"So you blamed yourself. That's why you left?"

Hazen nodded. "I figured Rick was working for Danielson. I'd seen them together and knew he was a militia member. I thought maybe if I could prove who did it and bring the creep in—"

Jeff ran both hands through his thick, dark hair. He was wearing it loose, Jennie noticed, like his father and his son.

"All right. Um—look, Jennie. I want to get your views on all this, but right now I need to talk to Hazen. You understand."

"Sure." Jennie felt relieved to be going. "If it's okay with you, I'd like to borrow a car and drive into Cottonwood to get this cast changed. It's getting pretty rank." She met Jeff's gaze. "I—um—thought maybe I'd stop at the jail on the way and talk to Eric and run a couple of errands. That is if it's okay with you."

Jeff handed her the camera lens and barrette. "Maybe you could drop these off at the sheriff's office—tell him what you told me. I'll call and let him know you're coming. We wouldn't want to be cited for withholding evidence."

"Okay." Jennie took the items and started to leave.

Joseph stopped her at the door. "Would you like me to go with you?"

Jennie glanced back at Hazen and Jeff. "If you want, but I'll be fine. It looks like those two need you more than I do right now. Oh, should I tell the sheriff about the mine?" She stopped, remembering Hazen didn't know about the mine yet. "I mean, with Eric taking the pages out of the diary and all."

"I don't think we need to reveal its whereabouts just now. But tell him that Eric must have heard the old legend about the mine and was looking for a map. Only, to our knowledge, there is no map." Joseph patted her shoulder and gave her a knowing smile.

"Mine?" Hazen's confused gaze darted from Jennie to Joseph. "What mine?"

Jennie didn't stick around to hear the explanation.

After a shower, clean clothes, and a quick hair-braiding session with Maggie and Amber, Jennie borrowed the white Jeep she'd ridden in when she'd first arrived. Since Maggie had called in to make an appointment for Jennie with Doctor Clark, their family doctor, the cast replacement went off without a hitch. Well, almost. Jennie had to listen to a half-hour lecture about what to do and what not to do when wearing a cast.

At eleven-thirty Jennie escaped the clinic and walked a block and a half up main street to the municipal building. Sheriff Mason rose to greet her when she entered. The office was actually one big room that held four desks and a high counter that stretched all the way across the room, separating the officers and their staff from the visitors. A half door at the far end provided the only access. A deputy sat at one desk, and a clerk—a woman in her forties whose nameplate read Sandy Mason—occupied another. The sheriff's wife?

"Well, well, if it isn't our little celebrity detective. Jeff White Cloud tells me you have some information for me." Sheriff Mason walked to the counter and rested his elbows on it.

Jennie ignored his condescending smile and handed him the lens and Heather's feather barrette. As she offered explanations, she almost wished she could find indisputable evidence to prove him wrong about Eric. That might knock him off his arrogant throne.

Only she had nothing at this point and Eric had confessed to the break-in. So, she offered up a quick prayer that Mason lose the next election.

When she'd finished her version of the break-in and Hazen's discovery, the sheriff rubbed his chin and stared at something on the other side of the room. "So, Hazen found his sister's barrette out at Jake's hunting lodge."

"Yes. I know he should have left it out there, but . . ."

"Somebody's going through a lot of trouble to make Jake look bad. I'm beginning to wonder if your uncle is behind all this."

"That's ridiculous."

"Is it? Jeff White Cloud has a long history as a political activist. Some of these guys will stop at nothing to get what they want. Just recently we've seen where some environmentalists have falsified records to sway public opinion. What better way to destroy your strongest political opponent than by discrediting him in the public's eyes? Framing him for murder and kidnapping would do it, don't you think?"

Jennie opened her mouth to respond, but couldn't think of anything to say.

"You seem surprised. Well, little lady, maybe you're not such a sharp detective after all. Don't tell me you didn't know your uncle plans to run for the State Senate against Danielson next year."

"No, but that wouldn't—"

"Since you're intent on bein' involved in this investigation, maybe you ought to get some of your facts straight. Go on over to the bank and talk to Alex Dayton. He's your uncle's biggest backer. 'Course he'll probably pull out when he gets wind of my theory."

Jennie stared at him. "You actually think my uncle caused an explosion that cost him a leg or that he kidnapped his own daughter?"

"Wouldn't be the first time a criminal shot himself in the foot."

Jennie pressed her lips together, deciding it might be better to keep her angry thoughts to herself. "May I visit Eric before I go, please?"

"Why?" he demanded.

"He's my cousin's boyfriend. He worked for my aunt and

uncle. I'd like to ask him why he betrayed them like he did."

He eyed her a moment, then apparently dismissed her as harmless. Either that or he suspected she might get something out of Eric that he hadn't. "Well, I guess it wouldn't hurt."

After searching her and walking her through a metal detector to make certain she wasn't carrying a weapon or some sort of escape device, the deputy, a man in his mid-thirties whose name pin read Luke Nelson, led her into a small cubicle with a glass partition down the middle. She sat at a table and waited. Five minutes later, the sheriff hauled Eric in and shoved him into the chair.

Eric's face contorted with pain. Jennie thought the rough handling unnecessary—especially when Eric had suffered a gunshot wound only yesterday.

"You got ten minutes," Sheriff Mason said, then left the room. Deputy Nelson stood at the door, rigid and unsmiling.

"Hi." Jennie leaned toward Eric and spoke into the speaker vent in the glass partition.

Eric stared at the table. He bore little resemblance to the handsome young photographer she'd met only a few days before. His unshaven face and messy hair made him look like a criminal. *Maybe that's because he is one, McGrady.*

Jennie ignored her impressions, deciding she'd better get to the point. "I heard you confessed. Why did you break into Joseph's cabin?"

Eric focused his hard blue gaze on her. "Why do you care? I admitted to doing it, isn't that enough?"

"No. Heather has been kidnapped, but then you knew that, didn't you?"

His gaze softened. "Yeah, I heard. Sheriff keeps telling me I did it." He shook his head. "I'd never hurt Heather. I love her."

"But you did break into her grandfather's cabin."

"I said I did. I was looking for something."

"A map?"

"Yeah." He frowned. "How did you know about that?"

"It doesn't matter. What I want to know is why."

Eric glared at her, then broke eye contact. "Heather told me about the mine. She wanted to find the map. I don't know what she thought she'd do with it. Maybe take some of the gold with her to California. I told her I had mon—" His gaze darted back to Jennie.

He was lying. Heather didn't know about the mine. At least Joseph hadn't told her. And where would he have gotten the idea there was a map? "Where is Heather now?"

"I don't know."

"She was going to meet you yesterday morning."

Eric closed his eyes. "I . . . she changed her mind. Said we should wait."

"And you got mad. Where is she, Eric?"

"I don't know, honest. I was going to leave as soon as I got my money—" He paused as if he'd said too much, then added, ". . . my paycheck from Mrs. White Cloud. I was out at Joseph's when somebody snuck up on me. Hit me on the head—knocked me out. I don't remember a thing until I woke up in the hospital."

Jennie shook her head. "You're saying someone knocked you out then shot you? That doesn't make much sense to me."

"That's what happened."

"The sheriff said you were the gunman Amber and I surprised in the llama pasture, and that you stole Danielson's pickup then returned it later that evening. Is that true?"

"Yeah."

"Why?"

"I was mad at Heather's old man. Look, I wanted to get back at him for keeping Heather and me apart. Figured maybe he'd sell out if he had enough bad luck. Move back to New York."

"Where did you get the gun?"

"Enough with the questions. You're starting to sound like the sheriff."

Jennie winced. She wasn't sure what had gotten into her. She wasn't usually so aggressive. But pieces of the puzzle were finally starting to slip into place.

"I'd just like some answers. You may love Heather, but you're more in love with the money you stand to inherit if she marries you. But that wasn't enough. Someone hired you to finish the job Rick Jenkins botched—to get the White Clouds to sell their land. Who might that be? Chad Elliot? Jake Danielson?"

"You're way off base. That explosion happened before I got here. I'm not working for anybody."

"I say you are and I'm going to keep digging until I find out who that is. What I don't understand is your loyalty to this person. They've kidnapped Heather, for Pete's sake, and shot you. If I were you I wouldn't go to jail for someone else's crimes. I'll bet the prosecutor would be willing to cut a deal if you told them who's behind this operation." Jennie leaned back, rather pleased with her performance.

Eric shook his head. "Come off it. You've been watching too much television. The only people paying my wages are the White Clouds, so give it a rest." Eric stood and signaled the deputy.

Jennie felt sorry for Eric. Someone was using him. She could see it in his eyes. "*Always watch the eyes when you question people*," Gram had told her. "*They say so much more than words*." Eric had expressive eyes. In their brief meeting he'd revealed his love for Heather, his guilt and shame for the crimes he'd committed. And fear. Part of what he'd told her had been the truth and part of it a lie. She needed to sort it all out.

The deputy ushered Jennie down the hall and through the office area. A well-dressed man in his late twenties was standing at the counter talking to Sally Mason. "You tell the sheriff I want to see him as soon as possible. I'm still staying at Marsha's Bed & Breakfast."

"You just missed him, Mr. Elliot," Sally said. "I'll let him know as soon as he comes in—unless it's urgent—then I can get him on the cellular."

"No, it'll wait."

So this was the famous Chad Elliot. Funny, he didn't look nearly as sinister as she'd pictured him. "Hello, Mr. Elliot." Jennie walked through the half door to his side of the counter.

Elliot frowned. "Do I know you?"

"Jennie McGrady. I'm Maggie and Jeff White Cloud's niece."

"I remember hearing about you." He smiled and opened the door, waited for her to exit, then stepped outside. "How's your uncle doing? It's a shame about his leg."

"He's better." Jennie wished she could think of something intelligent and witty to say. *Where do you fit into all this?* she wanted to ask. "And what do you need to see the sheriff about?" The thought slipped out. Too late, Jennie snapped her mouth shut and must have turned a dozen shades of red.

"What did you say?"

"I was just curious about your wanting to see the sheriff, that's all."

"That's none of your business." His annoyance melted into concern. "Look, Miss McGrady—um Jennie. I know the White Clouds hold me responsible for the explosion and all that's happened out at Dancing Waters, and now this kidnapping thing. I've had nothing to do with any of it."

"How do you explain the ransom note in Eric's pocket asking that Dancing Waters be deeded back over to you?"

Chad shook his head. "Do you honestly think I'd send a ransom note with my name on it? I do want the ranch back, but I fight my battles in court."

And with hired hit men, Jennie thought. "Did you hire Eric Summers?"

"Who? Oh, you mean the man who was shot yesterday. Sorry. I've never met him. I know you think of me as an adversary, but I'm really a nice guy."

That's what they all say.

Elliot glanced at his watch. "Have you had lunch?"

"No. I was just going to grab a hamburger."

"Then let me buy you one. There's a place around the corner that serves buffalo burgers."

"Buffalo?"

"You've never had it?"

"No." Jennie winced. "And I'm not sure I want to. But I had ostrich the other day and loved it, so why not?" As they walked Jennie chided herself for accepting his offer. *This guy could be dangerous, McGrady.* She ignored the warning and excused her actions on the basis that Chad Elliot might have information pertinent to the investigation.

She just hoped he didn't have anything more sinister on his mind than feeding her buffalo.

21

Jennie folded herself onto the seat of a picnic table in front of the Burger Barn. "Thanks," she said as Elliot set a large burger, fries, and a Diet Coke in front of her. He sat opposite her with the identical fare. She tried not to look surprised when he bowed his head and said grace.

Jennie lifted the burger to her mouth. Elliot watched as she took the first bite. "Good, huh?"

She nodded. "Mmmm."

"This is one of the original eating places in Cottonwood. My great-grandfather, Frank Elliot, practically built this town."

"I know. Joseph told me a lot about him. Sounds like he was a wonderful person."

"It blows me away to think about it sometimes. Frank settled here back in 1861. These are my roots. Ever since I was a little kid I dreamed of coming home to Dancing Waters." He stopped to take another bite of his burger, then went on, "Do you know how Dancing Waters got its name?"

Jennie nodded while she finished a French fry. "Joseph told me. It's such a sad story."

"I wish I'd talked to him before all this happened. Now that I've been established as 'the enemy' I'll probably never hear the full story. My lawyer started proceedings before I knew much of anything about the history of the place."

"Why don't you talk to him anyway? Joseph is one of the nicest and wisest men I've ever met. I'm sure he'd be happy to tell you about your family."

"I'd like to, but Bennett, that's my lawyer, says I shouldn't." He sighed. "I never could understand why my father left. Our roots are here and I had to come back."

She'd been wrong about Chad Elliot, Jennie realized. She'd judged and convicted him without hearing his side. "It must have been a shock to discover the land had been sold."

"Shock? That's putting it mildly. I was angry and hurt when the lawyer contacted me, so I decided to fight for what was rightfully mine. I'm not after all that much, you know. Just enough land to raise horses and a few head of cattle. I want to get married someday and rear my children here. . . ."

"What if you lose? What if you find out that Dancing Waters really does belong to Joseph? What will you do?"

He gave her a look of surprise. "White Cloud owns the land free and clear. I'm not contesting that."

"I don't understand. If you're not disputing ownership, what are the lawsuit and criminal charges about?"

"When I first found out about the land deal, I thought Joseph had taken advantage of my grandfather's alcoholism and had swindled him. But that wasn't the case. My grandfather sold the land with the idea of being able to buy it back someday. He died before he had the opportunity. Daniel—my father—didn't care. I do. All I'm asking for is the right to buy back part of the land Joseph plans to deed over to the park service. I still don't understand what the problem is. The bank has offered to loan me a hundred percent of the purchase price. It'll be a big mortgage, but I'm sure I can handle it."

"You just want to buy some of the land back? Do Joseph and Jeff know that?" Jennie doubted it.

"I assumed so. My lawyer's been negotiating with the White Clouds for months." He looked at his watch again. "I must be going. Thanks for listening. You're the first person I've actually talked to about my agenda other than my lawyer."

"I still think you should talk to Jeff and Joseph yourself. I have a feeling your lawyer may not be representing your best interests."

He grinned. "Now I don't feel so bad. You're suspicious of everyone, aren't you? But don't worry. I had Greg Bennett checked out before I hired him. He's well thought of in the community. His great-grandfather was one of the founding fathers. I'll talk to him, though—make sure we're communicating on the same level." He gathered their trash, dumped it in a nearby container, then waved good-bye. "Give my regards to your family."

Jennie walked the block and a half from the Burger Barn to the Cottonwood Historical Society. Now she could narrow down her list of suspects by one. Unfortunately, she had to add another—Greg Bennett. Bennett. Hmm. She dug into her memory, knowing she'd heard his name in another context. Nadi's diary. The Reverend Joshua Bennett. Could the lawyer be a relative? Had the Reverend passed the secret of the mine down to his sons and grandsons?

Cottonwood's historical society was housed in the Dayton Mansion. Myrtle Dayton, a white-haired volunteer who had to be at least eighty, greeted Jennie at the door. "Oh, do come in. You're my first visitor today. What can I do for you?"

"I'd like some information on Cottonwood back in the late 1800s—like the people who lived here then and who still have relatives living here today. Some information about the—"

"Wait," Mrs. Dayton interrupted. "Let me show you around the house first. It has a fascinating history. I grew up here, and when my parents died I donated it to the citizens of Cottonwood. It has most of the original furniture and looks much like it did when my grandfather Alexander Dayton had it built in 1895."

"Are you related to Alex Dayton, at the bank?" Jennie asked.

"He's my nephew." She pointed to a little boy in a family portrait. "There. My brother's son. Such a sweet boy. I live with him and his family."

"Is that his sister standing next to him?" Jennie asked.

Myrtle nodded. "Melissa is a Bennett now. Both of the children married well. My how the time flies. It seems like only yesterday I was changing their diapers and now their children are almost grown."

"Melissa Bennett? Greg Bennett's wife?" Jennie asked.

"Why, yes. Fine family. His father and grandfather were both ministers."

"Was his grandfather the Reverend Joshua Bennett?"

Myrtle gave her a look of surprise. "As a matter of fact, he was."

Excitement shivered up her spine. Now she was getting somewhere. Greg Bennett must have found out about the mine from his grandfather. What was it Chad had said—that Bennett had contacted him? She could hardly wait to get back to the ranch and report her findings to Jeff and Joseph.

As they were walking through the kitchen, Jennie heard a scraping noise that seemed to be coming from the basement. "What's that?" Jennie asked.

"Oh, I'm so embarrassed. It appears we have squirrels or some such animal." She shuddered. "I've called the exterminator and he should be out this afternoon."

Obviously embarrassed, Myrtle hurried Jennie out of the kitchen into the gift shop, where she helped Jennie pick out several books, journals, and pamphlets about the area and the early settlers. She gave Jennie photocopies of family trees—Elliot, White Cloud, VonHassen, Danielson, Mason, Dayton, Bennett, and any other families with roots going back into the late 1800s. Myrtle even loaned her a set of tapes telling the history of the area, which Jennie planned to listen to on her way back to the ranch.

"There are so many stories, dear. It's wonderful that a girl your age would take an interest in the past. So many don't, you know. My grandchildren, for example, haven't the vaguest interest. Except for Carey—that's Melissa's little girl. I have a feeling she'll end up being a lawyer like her daddy." She sighed. "There I go, rambling on again."

When she finally left the Dayton Mansion, Jennie's brain felt as sluggish as an out-of-memory computer. Jennie had a hunch the past played an important role in the case and only by unraveling it would the crimes of the present make sense. She needed a clear view of how their lives had connected and intertwined then and now.

On her way back to the car her certainty of Greg Bennett's guilt began to waver. She thought again about her talk with Chad Elliot. Had Greg Bennett been misrepresenting him? The times she'd seen Bennett, he'd seemed abrupt and cool—except toward Maggie—when he'd been out at the ranch. The way he'd talked, Jennie had gotten the impression he and his wife and Jeff and Maggie were friends. A moment ago she'd been ready to close the case, now she wasn't so sure.

Jennie's thoughts were interrupted by protests of two men standing on the steps outside the sheriff's office.

"Luke, you have to stop him." Alex Dayton followed the deputy down the steps. "Surely there's been some mistake. Sam can't be serious."

" 'Fraid so. I'm supposed to meet him out at Dancing Waters. He's called for armed backup in case there's trouble." Luke ducked into a squad car and peeled out.

"What's going on?" Jennie asked breathlessly as she came alongside Dayton. "What's he talking about?"

Dayton looked at her with a dazed expression—as if she

were the last person he'd expected to see. After a moment's hesitation, he said, "Do you believe in God, Jennie?"

"Sure. Why?"

"Then you'd better start saying your prayers. If I know Sheriff Mason, he's got an army of deputies out there. Most of them are members of the militia group, and there isn't a one that wouldn't like to see Jeff White Cloud dead."

"The militia—can't we stop them?" Jennie gasped. A mass of knots settled in her stomach.

"I'm afraid not. We'll just have to hope Jeff gives up without a fight. Somehow I don't think that's gonna happen."

"The sheriff's gone to arrest him?"

"That's right."

"On what charge?" The sheriff had speculated about Jeff, but as far as she knew he didn't have any proof.

"I'm not sure. Conspiracy, fraud, maybe even murder. He thinks White Cloud is behind the whole thing. Even set up the explosion."

"But that's not possible."

"I didn't think so either, but sometimes people aren't what they seem. The sheriff mentioned the possibility of Jeff's involvement and told me I'd be wise to pull my financial support."

Jennie stared at the man. How could he be thinking of money at a time like this? "Excuse me, Mr. Dayton. I need to find a way to stop Sheriff Mason. I have a pretty good idea now of who's behind this, and it is not my uncle."

Jennie jogged to a pay phone about half a block away. She fumbled with the tattered phone book, hunting through the yellow pages for the number of the state patrol, the FBI, anything but the sheriff's department.

"Oh no," she mumbled. As was the case at most pay phones, half the pages had been torn out. She tore open her bag and retrieved some change.

"Excuse me, but you seem to be rather frazzled. Can I

help you with something?" Alex Dayton asked.

Jennie jumped. "Oh, I didn't see you."

"I'm sorry if I startled you. I was just on my way back to the bank."

"I need to call the state patrol or someone to let them know what the sheriff is doing."

"You said something a few minutes ago about knowing who's behind all this. Have you been investigating?"

"Yes. But I don't have time to talk about it. Do you have some change I could borrow?"

He reached in his pocket and pulled up a couple of dimes and a few pennies. "Sorry, but I do have a phone. The bank is just across the street, why don't you use one of the phones over there?"

Within a few minutes Jennie was sitting in Alex Dayton's executive chair, dialing the State Patrol. She explained her concerns to the operator, then again to a man she assumed was an officer.

"Thank you for calling, Miss McGrady," he said when she finished. "We'll take your complaint about the sheriff's department under consideration. I'll pass the information along and have an officer get back to you." Before Jennie could argue, the man hung up.

Jennie slammed the phone down.

"Having trouble?" Dayton came back into the office.

"Yes. They said they'd get back to me." She looked up another number and dialed Joseph's cabin.

"Who are you trying now?"

"Joseph. Maybe he went back home. He'll know what to do." Jennie wished the banker would leave, but couldn't very well ask him to mind his own business. It was his office. Besides, he seemed as concerned about the situation as she did.

"No problem. I've got to lock up—I'll be back in a few minutes." Dayton left, closing the door behind him.

Joseph didn't answer. Frustrated, Jennie hung up. She

placed her cast on the desk and in the process of standing, knocked off a pile of papers that had been precariously stacked near the edge.

"Clumsy," Jennie muttered as she stooped to pick them up. She gathered the papers and reached for an envelope that had sailed under the chair. The name "Eric Summers" was written on it. Jennie lifted the flap and peered inside. Her heart beat a path to her throat.

Inside was a check signed by Jeff White Cloud made out to Eric Summers in the amount of ten thousand dollars. According to the date it had been drawn that day. She couldn't be certain, but the signature resembled the handwriting on the two death threats. Her heart stopped. Could the sheriff have been right after all? Had Jeff paid Eric to kidnap Heather? One thing she knew for certain—Eric did not make that kind of money taking photos and doing odd jobs on the ranch.

Wait a minute, McGrady, back up. What's the check doing in Mr. Dayton's office? Could this be some of the paper work he'd brought by the ranch yesterday? If so, he had to be involved somehow. The entire affair was beginning to look like a massive conspiracy. Jennie knew she couldn't rule out any suspects yet, but she just couldn't imagine her uncle being involved in something so sinister.

Jennie rummaged through the desk. In the third drawer down, buried beneath a stack of Dayton's stationery, she found two yellowed pages from Nadi's diary. Jennie left the evidence in place and eased the drawer closed.

The doorknob clicked and turned. Jennie slipped the check to Eric back into the envelope and buried it in the pile of papers. She'd been fast, but not fast enough. Dayton looked from the papers on the desk to her face.

Jennie's stomach lurched, threatening to set her buffalo burger free. "Some papers fell on the floor," she explained in what she hoped was a calm voice. "I was just picking them up for you."

"Is that right?" Their gazes collided. His kind blue eyes had turned an iron gray.

"You couldn't leave well enough alone, could you?"

"What do you mean?" Jennie feigned innocence, hoping she'd read him wrong.

Alex Dayton's eyes showed a trace of regret. He reached inside his suit jacket as if going for a gun. Jennie flinched—he was going to kill her.

22

She released the breath she'd been holding when he pulled out a white handkerchief and dabbed at his forehead and upper lip.

"Too bad," he said. "Now I'm going to have to alter my plans. But don't worry, it shouldn't prove too difficult. An accidental death should do it."

He walked toward her, stopping at a large oak cabinet near his desk. Jennie backed up and hit the wall. The window was open. Jennie thought about jumping through it.

"I wouldn't do that if I were you." He withdrew an automatic rifle from the cabinet and snapped in a cartridge.

Jennie sucked in a shallow breath and stared at the collection of at least a dozen weapons in his private arsenal—shotguns, pistols, even a crossbow. *This guy is supposed to be funding Jeff White Cloud's political campaign against the militia? That'd be like terrorists lobbying for gun control.*

Training the gun on her, he pawed through the papers on his desk and retrieved Eric's check. He waved the gun toward the door. "Let's go."

Jennie's hope moved up several notches. He couldn't possibly get her out of the building without being seen. She'd scream for help and dive behind a desk or something. Good plan. Bad timing. The bank was empty. So that's what he'd meant by locking up. "Where is everyone?"

"I gave them the rest of the day off with pay. We don't take tragedies lightly in this town. And a siege at Dancing Waters qualifies, don't you think? After all, several of my employees have family working out there."

Dayton ushered Jennie out the back door and shoved her into a waiting van—black with gold trim. She'd seen it out at Dancing Waters before and as soon as she stepped inside, realized who it belonged to.

Chad Elliot's lawyer, Greg Bennett, sat behind the wheel. "Hurry up."

Dayton jumped in, closed the sliding door, then grabbed a rope from under the passenger seat. He yanked Jennie's arms behind her.

"Ow. Take it easy." Jennie imagined herself yanking her arm out of his grasp and slamming the cast into his smug face.

"What are you doing?" The highly recommended lawyer started the van.

"Tying her up. What else am I going to do with a rope, hang her?"

"Forget that. If the authorities find rope marks on her wrist they'll get suspicious. You'll just have to strap her in and keep an eye on her." He glanced at his watch. "Where is Summers? I thought you told him to meet us as soon as he got out."

"Don't worry. He'll be here. White Cloud posted bail nearly an hour ago. I've got his money. Which he won't get until he does this one last job for us."

Bennett laughed. "Don't you mean for White Cloud?"

"Of course. Everything leads back to White Cloud." Dayton handed the gun to his partner and climbed into the front seat. He swiveled around, took the gun back, and trained it on Jennie.

"Here he comes." Bennett lowered the power window a

couple of inches. "It's about time. Get in the back and keep an eye on our guest."

Bennett had the van rolling before Eric could sit down. He swung around and dropped into the seat beside her.

Surprise registered on his face, then anger. "What's she doing here? You hire her too?"

Jennie glared at him. "Not everyone has a price."

Eric caught her gaze, had the decency to look guilty, then glanced back at the two businessmen.

"Our snoopy young investigator here is about to be the victim of a few stray bullets," Bennett sneered. "Gunned down by one of the dozens of deputies combing the grounds."

"You're going to kill her?"

"No, you are."

"Why?"

"She knows too much." Dayton frowned. "When we get out to the ranch I'm going to turn you loose with this." He held up the weapon. "Pump about half a dozen bullets into her, then we're out of here. We'll take you up to the airport in Missoula."

Fear raced through her like a raging fire. *There has to be a way out, McGrady,* she told herself. *You've gotten out of tight spots before. Right, but he's got an automatic rifle and he's driving straight into a war zone.* Jennie could see the headlines now: "Teenager Accidentally Killed in Indian Massacre at Dancing Waters."

When she'd been trapped in the mine she'd experienced a strange and welcome peace. And earlier when she'd been lost in the woods, Joseph had reminded her to be still. God had been faithful to bring her this far. With the faith of her grandmother and Joseph, Jennie took a deep breath and swallowed back the rising terror. She leaned back against the seat. Somehow she'd find a way out of this.

"You got my money?" Eric asked.

Dayton patted his breast pocket. "And the deed to your new condominium in Fort Lauderdale. All courtesy of Jeff White Cloud."

Eric nodded and stared straight ahead, his mouth set in a hard line. He'd cleaned up before getting out of jail and looked like Heather's handsome young photographer friend again.

How ironic, Jennie thought. *On the outside, they look like the professionals they claim to be.* Success oozed out of every thread in their expensive clothes. But inside they were nothing but slime.

"Everyone has a dark side," Gram had told her. *"We are all capable of good and evil. The weakest of us are those who allow the evil to control them."*

The men's voices broke in on her thoughts.

"Did you ever find the map?" Bennett asked.

Dayton shook his head. "I was sure it would be in the old man's house. Even looked in his and Jeff's safety deposit boxes at the bank—nothing."

The mine. Jennie had an idea. It would mean revealing Joseph's secret and disclosing its whereabouts. She hesitated a moment. Should she? What would Joseph say? Since it seemed her only chance for escape, Jennie felt certain Joseph and Uncle Jeff would approve. "There is no map."

Bennett peered at her through the rearview mirror. "And just how would you know that?"

"Joseph told me."

"You're lying!" Eric snapped. "Back at the jail—"

"I mentioned the map because I wanted more information from you. I had a hunch that's what you were looking for because of the missing pages in Nadi's diary. I also knew you were lying when you said Heather told you about the mine. She didn't know about it."

Jennie turned her attention back to the two men in the front seat. "But then that's why you kidnapped her, isn't it?

Were you going to have her lead you to the mine? Did you offer to pay her off too? And when she refused you—"

Dayton silenced Jennie with a steel gray stare. "You ask too many questions."

"I know—it's a habit." Jennie struggled to maintain a sense of calm. She had to make them think she was tough. "Look, you're going to kill me anyway, so why not satisfy my curiosity. Where's Heather? Eric already told me she'd changed her mind about going with him."

When no one answered, Jennie leveled an accusing gaze on Eric. "Is that when you decided to kidnap her? Or had that been part of the plan? What I don't understand, Eric, is how you could still cover for these guys. I mean, they shot you and abducted Heather."

"I'll heal. They promised they wouldn't hurt her." Eric closed his eyes. "Besides, she doesn't know anything. Eventually she'll get my letter and find out that her dad hired me and that the kidnapping thing was all a ruse to discredit Elliot."

Jennie shook her head. "This is the craziest scheme I've ever heard. You can't possibly get away with it."

"I'm afraid we can," Dayton said. "You see, Jennie, we're the only ones above suspicion in this deal. Eric's letter to Heather and the fact that White Cloud paid his bail was all the proof Sheriff Mason needed. In the end, Danielson, White Cloud, and Elliot will all be dead. Dancing Waters will revert back to the bank, go up for auction, and be sold to the highest bidders. Which, of course, will be myself and Greg. We'll be buying it out of a deep sense of loss for our dearly departed friends."

Eric stiffened beside her. His eyes widened and his Adam's apple moved up and down as he swallowed. He had to know they wouldn't let him leave. He knew even more than she did about their plans.

Bennett made a right onto a gravel road. It was one that

she'd taken that morning with Joseph. It ran between the Danielsons' ranch and Dancing Waters. Jennie decided it was time to put her plan into action. "Maybe I was wrong about not having a price," Jennie said. "I know where the mine is. Maybe we can make a deal."

Bennett braked. The van spun out on the loose gravel and the lawyer almost lost control. He managed to right the vehicle, stopped it, and whipped around in his seat.

"What kind of deal?" both men asked at once.

"Well, I might be persuaded to take you there for, say, half a million dollars. I might even be persuaded to go home with a case of amnesia for say—another half mil."

Bennett and Dayton looked at each other. "We might be willing to work something out," Bennett said, "but only if the mine's as rich as my grandfather said it was."

"Oh, it's rich all right. There's a foot-wide vein of pure gold not more than fifteen feet from the entrance." Jennie dug into her pocket and handed the nugget to Dayton. "I picked this up off the mine floor. I was going to have it assayed, but Joseph assured me it was the real thing."

Dayton fingered the gold, weighed it in the palm of his hand, and bit into it. "She's right."

Jennie shuddered at the look in his eyes. Greed. She'd seen it before and knew it had the power to turn people into savages.

"Where is it?" Bennett asked.

"Just keep driving," Jennie said. "I'll tell you where to stop. We'll have to hike into the woods a ways."

"What do you think, Alex?" Bennett started the van and pulled back onto the road. "She being straight with us?"

"We'll know soon enough. It'll put us a little behind schedule, but that shouldn't matter now."

They drove on in silence. Dayton still faced toward the back, with his gun at the ready. Eric kept looking at her, his eyes sending repentant messages to let her know he wanted out.

It was a little late for that, but Eric would be a valuable witness against Dayton and Bennett. Maybe she should bring him with her when she made her escape. Maybe not. Eric may have been scared straight, but Jennie just plain didn't trust him.

"Pull off on the other side of the bridge," Jennie said.

"Are you sure?" Bennett asked, braking and coming to a stop at a wide spot in the road where the bridge ended.

"Yes. I haven't come in this way, but we'll follow the creek up. You'll need a flashlight for when we go into the mine."

She led the three men along the creek bank. The water had receded, leaving mud and debris in its path. "Those aren't the best shoes for hiking." Jennie suppressed a snicker as Dayton slipped down the bank into the creek. By the time they reached the meadow below the mine, both men looked like they'd been mud wrestling. She and Eric didn't look much better, but that didn't matter. Soon she'd be free.

On the hike in, Jennie replayed her escape scene over and over in her head—had it planned out to the second. She just hoped the men wouldn't kill her before she got them into the mine.

23

Jennie held her breath as she climbed up the familiar hill-side.

"There's nothing up here," Bennett said, panting heavily. He stopped about a fourth of the way up. "She's just trying to wear us out so she can get away."

Dayton, red-faced and looking as if he might have a heart attack at any moment, paused to catch his breath. "Let's go." He nudged Bennett, then started climbing again.

"It's just a little farther." Had Jennie known what poor physical condition they were in, she might have tried running, but they had a powerful gun and she doubted she could have outrun the bullets.

She reached the mine's entrance and stopped. Eric was right behind her, the others about thirty yards behind.

"What are you going to do?" Eric whispered.

"Show them the mine."

"You mean it's really up here?"

Jennie nodded.

"I know you're up to something. I want to help. Look, remember what you said earlier at the jail about getting a lighter sentence? Maybe—" Eric stopped as Dayton and Bennett caught up with them.

Bennett leaned against an outcropping of rock. "I told you she was lying. There's no mine."

"It's hidden." Jennie moved aside the brush and pushed the lever. As before, the door shuddered open. She ducked inside.

"Well I'll be." Still panting, Dayton pushed Eric in ahead of him. Bennett followed, switching on the flashlight as he entered.

"The vein I told you about is back here. I'll show you." Jennie rushed ahead of them. She stopped and pointed, then stepped out of the way.

Bennett shined the flashlight on the gold and both men gasped in greedy delight. "She was right."

"Woo-wee," Dayton whooped. "I've never seen anything like it."

While the gold enticed the men, Jennie backed out of the circle of light toward the entrance. Any second the door would close, trapping them inside. Near the entrance now, she listened for the click. When she heard it, she spun around and dove through the opening. She could hear bullets ping as they hit the inside of the metal door.

Jennie scrambled to her feet. That's when she discovered her escape hadn't gone quite as smoothly as she'd hoped. Eric winced as he sat up. He rubbed his arm just below the bullet wound, then reached up to pull some twigs from his hair. "Wow! That was some escape."

"How did you know what I was going to do?"

"I didn't. I just followed your lead." Favoring his injured arm, he stood and brushed the dirt from his jeans. "Look, Jennie. What I did was wrong. I should have gone to Jeff as soon as Dayton contacted me. I didn't do it just for the money. They threatened to hurt Heather. I shouldn't have listened. He and Bennett may have already killed her."

"You better hope not." Jennie picked up a rock and jammed it against the lever. Even if Bennett and Dayton discovered how to open it from the inside, they wouldn't be able to get out—she hoped.

"What now?" Eric asked.

Though Jennie still didn't fully trust him, she wasn't afraid of him either. If she could have managed it, she'd have handcuffed him to a tree and left him for the sheriff, but that wasn't an option. "I'm heading back to the ranch. I'd suggest you come along and turn yourself in." Without waiting for an answer, Jennie raced down the hill toward the creek. She had to stop the sheriff and his deputies. She just hoped it wasn't too late.

"Jennie, wait up," Eric panted as Jennie started to cross the creek. "Where are you going?"

"Back to the ranch. Are you coming or not?"

"Why don't we take the van?"

Jennie stopped and spun around. "It would be quicker, but the keys—" She paused as he held them up, grinning like he'd pulled off a major coup. "When did you. . . ?"

"While they were busy keeping an eye on you. Come on, let's go." He took off running toward the road where the van sat waiting.

When they arrived at the dude ranch twenty minutes later, an ambulance with sirens and lights engaged pulled away from the lodge. Jennie didn't want to think about who might be in it—or how many more there'd be.

The ambulance was the only sign of trouble. The ranch looked much as it had when Jennie had first arrived. Guests milled around and ostriches stared at her from the security of their pen. Sheriff Mason was standing on the porch outside the lodge office shaking Jeff's hand as though they'd just finished coffee.

Maggie, who'd been standing between Jeff and Chad Elliot, spotted her, ran down the steps, and threw her arms around Jennie's neck. "Thank God you're safe." She stepped back and frowned. "You're filthy. What happened? And what's Eric doing here?"

"It's a long story," Jennie said. "But . . . I'm confused. I thought the sheriff had come out here with Danielson's militia group to arrest Uncle Jeff. I expected the place to look like a war zone."

Chad Elliot came down the steps toward her. "I think I can help you out there, Jennie. After you and I talked, I got to thinking about what you said and decided to take your advice. Came out to talk to the White Clouds myself. And it's a good thing I did. I was here when the sheriff and his deputies arrived. You were right, Bennett has been misrepresenting me from the beginning. We've been having a long talk about who might be behind all this."

"I'd better head on into town." Sheriff Mason adjusted his hat. "I still can't believe Bennett's our guy. But I'll follow up on your suspicions."

"Believe it, Sheriff," Jennie said. "Bennett's guilty—so is his brother-in-law."

"Alex?" Jeff stared at her as though she'd just grown another head. "I can't believe he'd be involved in something like this. Are you sure?"

"Positive. They developed this incredible plan to take over Dancing Waters. Only you won't find them in town, Sheriff." She gave him a brief accounting of what had happened.

"Let me get this straight." Sheriff Mason looked skeptical. "You trapped Bennett and Dayton in a gold mine?" He shook his head and laughed. "Now I've heard everything."

Eric, who'd been silent to that point stepped between Jennie and the sheriff. "She's telling the truth. They hired me to stir up trouble between the Danielsons and White Clouds. They hired Rick Jenkins too, only he messed up. They were going to make me kill Jennie. I—I'm willing to testify against them if—well, Jennie said if I testified I could get a lighter sentence."

"Is that right?" Sheriff Mason glowered at her, but Jennie thought she noted a sliver of respect. "Last time I looked, I was wearing the badge around here." He fussed a little more about people taking the law into their own hands, then asked a deputy to take Eric into town. After promising to make a concerted effort to find Heather, Mason followed Joseph to the mine to pick up Bennett and Dayton.

"Who was in the ambulance?" Jennie asked Maggie and Jeff after they'd gone.

Maggie pinched her lips together and squeezed Jennie's shoulder.

"Oh no, not Hazen?"

"No, honey. Hazen went into town to look for you. When you didn't come back we got worried. He should be calling in any time, and we'll let him know you're here."

"Then, who?"

"Jake Danielson. The excitement was too much for him. He had a heart attack."

"Is he dead?"

"No, at least he wasn't when he left."

Jennie felt relieved and sad at the same time. "Poor Marty." Jennie sank onto the steps and rested her head against a post.

Maggie sat down beside her. "You must be exhausted. Why don't you head up to the house, take a shower and rest for a while?"

"Can't." She yawned and let her eyes drift closed. Just for a minute. "I need to find Heather."

"Jennie McGrady." Maggie heaved an exasperated sigh and wrapped an arm around Jennie's shoulders. "No wonder your mother worries about you. You don't know when to quit."

Jennie didn't, but apparently her body did. Though she desperately wanted to look for Heather, she followed Maggie's orders and let Lopez drive her up to the house. After a quick shower, she went to bed.

When Jennie awoke, it was dark. A narrow strip of light

seeped out from under the closet door. After a few minutes, the light went out and the door opened. A slender figure emerged.

Jennie threw back her covers. "Don't tell me you're sneaking out again?"

"Oh," Heather squealed. "You scared me. I thought you were sleeping."

"I was. Now I'm awake." Jennie rubbed her eyes. "Wait a minute. Is this a dream? What are you doing here?"

"Sheriff Mason brought me home." Heather reached for the stained-glass lamp and turned it on. Rainbows of light splintered the darkness.

"Really? He found you? When?"

"He didn't find me. Hazen and Mrs. Dayton did."

Jennie rubbed her forehead. "Mrs. Dayton? But how—wait, don't tell me. Mr. Dayton hid you in the mansion. You were making the noises we heard."

"I heard your voice and tried to get your attention."

Jennie knocked herself alongside the head. "I can't believe it. I was so focused on the research I was doing, it didn't even occur to me that it might be you."

"Don't be so hard on yourself," Heather said. "If it hadn't been for you . . . well, you uncovered Dayton and Bennet's plot and caught them. You saved our lives."

Jennie's face warmed with the compliment. "You said Hazen and Mrs. Dayton found you?"

"Actually he was in town looking for you. Someone said they'd seen you go into the mansion. When I heard him, I made as much noise as I could. And . . . I called to him in my mind." She shrugged. "I know it sounds weird, but being twins we can sometimes hear each other's thoughts. Anyway, Hazen decided to check out the noises—and there I was."

"Are you okay? They didn't hurt you?"

"I'm fine. My wrists are sore and my mouth still hurts from the gag."

Jennie swung her legs off the bed and sat up all the way. "I'm really glad you're home. I was afraid they'd killed you."

"Yeah." Heather stood and walked to the door. "I have to go. Marty's waiting for me downstairs. Mom said if you were awake I should have you come down for dinner."

"You're going out with Marty?"

"I promised I'd go to the hospital with him to see his dad."

Jennie nodded. "Tell him hi."

"I will." Heather opened the door.

"Heather?" Jennie closed the distance between them and gave Heather a hug. "I'm so glad you're back."

Tears gathered in her cousin's eyes. "Me too."

Jennie flipped on the overhead light and got dressed. She felt strange—sort of unfinished. Maybe it was because she'd missed connecting Heather to the Dayton Mansion. "You can't win them all, McGrady," she told her mirror image as she brushed through her long tresses. Jennie tipped her head to one side and clipped on one of Heather's feathered barrettes. She may not have solved the case single-handedly, but Jennie took comfort in knowing that even if she hadn't survived her abduction, Bennett and Dayton would have been caught. Their plan had begun to unravel in too many places.

Jennie glanced toward the ceiling. "Thank you," she whispered, then headed downstairs.

24

Two days later, after one of Maggie's gourmet dinners, Jennie stretched out on the carpeted living-room floor between Nick and Amber and watched her mother and Maggie erase the years that had separated them.

Mom and Nick had flown in the day before. Jennie had driven up to Missoula to get them. They'd spent the entire drive catching up. After hearing about Hannah's grandparents and their home in Arizona, Jennie felt better about the little girl being there. Nick didn't. But his bad mood began to dissipate the minute Amber introduced him to the animals—especially the horses.

Jennie felt as if she'd already had a full day. The mid-morning ceremony had gone off without so much as a protest sign. In the headdresses and beaded buckskin of their ancestors, Joseph, Jeff, Hazen, Heather, and Amber presented the U.S. Forestry Service with ten thousand acres of prime land to be preserved for future generations.

Now, as Jennie watched their faces and felt their anticipation, she knew there was more excitement to come.

"Can't tell you how glad I am I talked to you," Chad Elliot told Jennie for the umpteenth time since dinner. "I just feel so gullible to have been taken in by those creeps."

"You mustn't blame yourself, Chad." Maggie perched on the arm of the chair in which her husband sat.

"We were all taken in." Jeff had exchanged the wheelchair for a pair of crutches. In another week or two, he'd be walking on his own.

"There is no deeper wound than the betrayal of a friend. It will take time for these wounds to heal. But I have something that may help." Joseph excused himself and came back a few moments later with an envelope.

Hazen, Heather, Maggie, and Jeff all looked at one another as though they were sharing a private joke.

"Chad," Joseph said as he sat back down. "You told us earlier you wished to have the opportunity to purchase back a portion of the land."

"Yes." He sighed. "But I'm not sure that will be possible now. I don't think I can get a loan from anyone else. I should have been suspicious of Dayton's motives when he offered to loan me such a large amount with so little collateral."

Joseph handed him an envelope. "We had a meeting to discuss your request and have come up with a plan we think will be acceptable to you."

Chad opened the envelope and pulled out an official-looking letter. Tears gathered in his eyes as he read. "I can't believe this. After all that's happened. I don't know what to say."

Curiosity got the better of Jennie. "What is it?"

Joseph chuckled. "Patience, Brave Eagle. You will know soon enough."

"You were absolutely right about these people, Jennie," Elliot said. "They've just given me the deed to the five hundred acres my great-grandfather gave White Cloud. I can't accept this, Joseph, it's your home."

"But, Papa, where will you live?" Amber asked.

"I am old, Tiponi. I don't have many years left. I will move into one of the guest houses."

His news delighted Amber. "Then I can see you every day?"

"Every day."

"Still," Elliot argued, "this is too much."

"There are a few stipulations," Jeff said. "Now that the mine is no longer a secret, and we can enforce laws to preserve the environment, we thought it might be best to reopen it. We've decided to ask you to oversee the mining operation. You'll receive a salary along with a share of the profits."

"I don't know what to say." Elliot glanced around the room.

"We'll work out the details later." Joseph nodded to Jeff. "Now we must give Jennie her reward for bringing Dayton and Bennett to justice."

"We're setting up a trust fund for you, Jennie," Jeff said. "A percent of the profits from the mine will go into an account bearing your name. Law school costs a lot of money and I want you to have the best."

Jennie glanced at her mother, expecting an objection. Mom just smiled. As Jennie looked from one person to the next, their faces faded behind a veil of tears. Her thank-yous barely made it past the baseball-size lump that clogged her throat. She circled the room and hugged them all.

———

A week later, they stood in the shadow of the Bitterroot Mountains saying a final good-bye to Jake Danielson. On top of his coffin Marty placed a crate of his father's guns. He removed his hat and bowed his head. "I loved my father. We didn't always agree, but he did right by me. By burying his guns with him, I'm not saying that my father's involvement in the militia was right or wrong. All I'm saying is The Double D is mine now and I got plans that don't include the use of weapons or military training. This is a ranch, pure and simple." He glanced up at the man wearing a clerical collar. "That's all I got to say."

The Reverend Pierce, who served at the church where the

Danielsons were members, took charge. "Let us pray. Our Father . . ."

After the funeral they all went back to Dancing Waters where Aunt Maggie and Mom served a buffet lunch and consoled Mrs. Danielson and the other mourners.

Jennie, Hazen, Marty, and Heather changed clothes, packed up their camping gear, and headed into the woods toward Crystal Hot Springs. Since this was Jennie's last night, they'd decided to spend it camping under the stars on Blue Ridge. "I wish you could stay longer, Jennie," Hazen said.

"Me too. I'm going to miss this place." Jennie scooped up a pine cone and threw it at a tree. "The mountains and trees, the horses—"

"What about us?" Hazen teased. "I know we're weird, but won't you miss us a little?"

"A lot. But I have a hunch we'll see each other more often now that our mothers have gotten back together."

"Why don't you come back next year?" Heather turned around and walked backward. "Stay for the whole summer." Although Heather had no intention of giving up modeling, she'd agreed to finish college and stay at Dancing Waters— a decision which had Marty Danielson's full approval.

"I think you should," Marty looped an arm around Heather's neck and grinned. "These guys need somebody to keep them out of trouble and I'm not sure I can handle the job myself."

"I might, provided they don't lure me into the woods and throw tomahawks at me."

"Naw." Hazen grinned and raised his eyebrows. "But we might be able to come up with something else. Like dumping a few spiders into your sleeping bag."

"You wouldn't."

"On the other hand, I'll probably be too busy to get into trouble."

"Yeah?"

"Dad and Gramps have taken me on as a partner. I'll be heading the new trailblazing unit."

"Which is—"

"We'll be taking guests on wilderness treks in the mountains and teaching them to respect and nurture the land."

"Tell them your Indian name, Hazen," Heather said. "Papa decided Hazen was ready."

"*Yuma*. It means 'chief's son.'"

"Congratulations, Yuma." Jennie flashed him a wide smile. She glanced from Hazen to Heather and back again. The three of them had been almost inseparable the last few days. And now Jennie didn't just count them as cousins, but friends. She had only one wish—that Lisa could be there with them. Maybe next time.

The following day it rained. Their flight went on as scheduled.

Jennie's sadness over leaving Dancing Waters turned into joy as they arrived in Portland. Her best friend and cousin was waiting at the gate.

"I can't wait to hear about your trip," Lisa said. "But first I've got to tell you what happened. Someone broke into the school and . . ."

Jennie sighed. *Forget it, McGrady. Don't even think about getting involved. This is one case you are going to ignore.*

Uh-huh, her adventurous spirit contradicted, *wanna bet?*